THE RAGE PLAGUE

A NOVEL BY
ANTHONY GIANGREGORIO

Permuted Press
The formula has been changed...
Shifted... Altered... Twisted.
www.permutedpress.com

As always there are a few special people who helped me finish this book.

Roger, as always, thanks for you support; I could use a few more friends like you. And of course thanks to my wife Jody, who is still my biggest fan and the first to read the finished product.

Also, my son Joseph helped immensely, searching for those insidious grammatical errors that seem to rise from the grave like newly awakened zombies.

And to my youngest son, Domenic, who is writing his own zombie book, though he's only completed one page. But that's okay; he has the rest of his life to finish it. The beginning of this book is based on his work, I liked it so much.

A **Permuted Press** book
published by arrangement with the author

ISBN-10: 1-934861-19-7
ISBN-13: 978-1-934861-19-6

Cover art by Chris Kaletka.
Edited by D.L. Snell.

10 9 8 7 6 5 4 3 2 1

CHAPTER 1

"They're gaining on us!" Bill Thompson yelled, heavy footsteps chasing him down the hallway past school photos and paintings from the second grade, reminders of how normal the world had been only a few days ago. Behind the footsteps, something growled, something like a hundred snarling wolves in pursuit.

Four other survivors ran behind him, each looking as bad as he felt. Elizabeth took the lead, followed by Janice and an old man in his late seventies. Walter, if Bill remembered right. Behind Walter was another woman, Kathy Myers. Bill remembered someone mentioning her name when he'd been introduced to the group. That had been three days ago—back when people first started attacking their neighbors.

Behind Bill and the others, twenty crazed people charged down the hall. He saw the first couple of psychos as they ran under one of the few working fluorescent lights, flapping their tongues like dogs, their eyes wild and mad as if whoever lived there had moved out, leaving only pure unadulterated rage.

Bill put on another burst of speed as he rounded a corner. His shoes slipped on the ceramic tile and he almost crashed to the floor; only a miracle kept him upright.

He just had to make it to the end of the hall. The ladder to the roof access was only a few yards away, and he knew he would make it the moment he turned the corner. He glanced over his shoulder. Walter was falling behind—he was too old. Kathy helped him along.

A few feet from the ladder, Bill stopped. Elizabeth and Janice ran by him and scurried up the metal rungs to the roof.

Bill watched the crazies gain on Walter and Kathy. "Hurry!" he screamed.

Kathy ran faster, dragging Walter behind her. It looked like they would reach Bill in time—until the two-inch heel on Kathy's high-priced shoe gave out.

She collapsed to the floor, dragging Walter down with her. Both screamed in surprise, and Bill heard Walter's hip break against the tile.

He hesitated for only a moment. The S&W .38 revolver in his hand would certainly deter a few crazies, but the others in the crowd wouldn't care. He decided he had no choice.

"I'm sorry," he said, and he sprinted towards the ladder. A small voice screamed that he should help them, that he was no better than the crazies if he left his friends to be torn apart and murdered, but his own fear, his own survival instinct forced the voice down.

Bill placed his feet on the bottom rungs and looked over his shoulder one last time. He could only watch as Walter and Kathy were buried in an avalanche of snarling bodies, as Kathy's yellow dress completely disappeared. Their screams filled the hallway, bouncing off the metal lockers to be lost amidst the growls of their attackers.

Briefly, a window opened between the bodies and Bill saw Kathy pull a pencil from somewhere on her person and jam it into the eye of a crazed man. He jumped on her anyway and continued to rip her apart, his eye now dripping white and pinkish ooze.

Bill looked away, sick. He scurried up the ladder just as the first crazy reached the bottom rungs. He rolled away from the hatch as a fellow survivor slammed it shut and slid a metal bar through the handle. The attackers banged on the underside, jostling the hatch with each punch.

Bill lay on his back, looking up at the few stars visible through the low cloud cover, barely feeling the loose gravel digging into his skin through his shirt. He breathed in heavy gasps, and for a second he wondered if he would finally have a heart attack.

During his last visit to the doctor's office, his tests had indicated high cholesterol and high blood pressure. It wasn't much of a surprise, of course. Just like more than seventy percent of America, he indulged in fast food and even faster snacks, chomping on pork rinds and potato chips till the cows came home. His doctor had advised him to watch his diet and start exercising before he suffered a heart attack or a stroke.

Bill chuckled, realizing he would be dead long before his heart gave out.

"What the hell's so funny?" Mike Fogarty asked; he was blond, in his late twenties—just a kid. "Where are Kathy and the old man?"

Bill looked up at him. "Nothing's funny, Mike. Not a damn thing."

Another woman came over to Bill. A light breeze blew her red hair across her face, and she brushed it away so she could see. "Come on, Bill, where's Kathy and the old man?"

He frowned long and deep, and with a moan he climbed to his feet. He was almost fifty, and at the moment every year was bearing down on him.

Bill placed his hands on the woman's shoulders and let out another deep sigh. He should have gone back for them. "I'm really sorry, Melissa, but those nutjobs found a way in on the north side. Kathy's shoe broke and she fell. She never had a chance, Walter either."

Melissa's face froze in shock, her eyes barely moving. Then she turned away and started to cry. Kathy had been her best friend for more than half her life.

Mike jabbed Bill with his finger, then pointed at the roof access. "Okay fine, that explains Kathy, but where's Walter? Did his shoe break too?"

Bill pushed the kid away and held up his hand to keep him at arm's length. "Hey, who risked their asses to close all the doors and get food from the cafeteria, huh, Mike? I didn't see *you* down there. I told you Walter was too damn old, but would you listen to me? Hell no! Now Kathy's dead!"

Mike wasn't about to give in, but an older woman stepped between them. Her name was Marie Connelly and she had arrived at the school with Walter. They'd been friends.

Marie's gray hair never moved from the stiff breeze on the roof, held in place with hairspray. She wore a pair of large eyeglasses over her small eyes, and when she smiled she reminded people of their grandmother.

"All right, you two, that's enough. Now, Mike," she said soothingly, "Walter wanted to go with them and he was too stubborn to listen. It's just a shame that Kathy had to go down with the old fool."

Mike wasn't about to give in that easily. Ever since he'd arrived a day after Bill, he had been gunning for lead man of their little survival group. He felt he could do a better job than Bill and tried to undermine him at every opportunity. He didn't understand why everyone else followed him.

Bill could have cared less who was in charge, as long as he wasn't expected to risk his own life. If the others wanted him to lead, he was happy to go along with it.

Mike pointed to the gun in Bill's hand. "Fine, Marie, if you want to stick up for him, then you know I can't stop you, but what about the gun? Why didn't he use it to save them?"

Bill spit onto the roof and took another step forward. "Because there were too damn many of them, you dumb shit! Even if I'd tried, they would've got me too. The crazy bastards aren't scared of anything, you know that!"

Marie turned to Mike and stepped closer to him. "He's got a point, Mike. And as soon as you calm down you'll realize he did the right thing."

Mike was about to argue when his girlfriend Becky walked up to him and grabbed his hand. "Come on, honey, that's enough for now. I'm lonely." Becky was in her early twenties with a figure that would make any man drool. Her blond hair reached down her back and caressed the top of her jeans. Her blue eyes would make any man melt, and she knew it. She used those same eyes now to pull Mike away from the others.

"Please, baby." She bit her lower lip and cooed softy. "Come keep me company. I'm cold and I need you to keep me warm."

Gently, she pulled him away, but he slowed and looked Bill square in the face, pointing at him with his right finger. "This ain't over, old man, not by a long shot." Then he gave in and let his girlfriend lead him to another part of the school roof.

Bill looked to Marie and grinned. "Thank you, Marie. I don't know what I'd do without you."

She chuckled. "You don't? I would think the answer to that is obvious. Either you or him would have to knock the other on his butt and settle your little feud."

Bill brought his hand to his chest and smiled sheepishly. "Me? I'm innocent in all of this and you know it."

She nodded. "Perhaps, but you could still listen a little when the man talks. He may be young, but he has a good head on his shoulders. You shouldn't be so quick to dismiss him when he suggests something."

Bill looked out onto the street along the front of the school. "Please, that boy has some serious daddy issues to work out, and if you don't mind I'd rather not be his surrogate. He's an arrogant bastard."

"Perhaps, Bill. But maybe he respects you more than you think and he's just too afraid to admit it. Have you ever thought of that?"

Bill frowned. He hadn't thought of it actually. He resolved to listen more to Mike the next time they had a problem.

With a sigh, Bill walked over to the rest of the survivors huddling around the gravel roof. He couldn't remember all their names. They had all come to the school, as pairs or alone, to hide from the crazies, hoping that sooner or later the police or National Guard would straighten up the mess.

A teenage boy, maybe twelve or thirteen, sat quietly against an air conditioning unit. His younger brother leaned against him, no more than four or five. At the beginning of the outbreak, the poor children had watched their father kill their mother. The dad came after them too, but they locked themselves in their bedroom and crawled out the window. It was amazing they'd survived in the streets long enough to find sanctuary at the school.

As Bill looked down at the two boys, their names finally came back to him. The older one was Roger and the other was Phillip.

Next to them was another man. He was about thirty or so and he stared out over the roof. He hadn't uttered a single word since arriving, but just followed orders and sat quietly when he wasn't needed. Bill suspected that the man had lost his wife because when he first arrived he'd been carrying a bloody picture of a woman. It had been pretty easy to figure out what must have happened.

There were a few other survivors, both men and women he didn't know. They didn't have much time for socializing.

It was midsummer, and a cool, comfortable breeze blew over the roof. He wasn't looking forward to tomorrow when the sun would bake their heads. The gravel on the roof would only amplify the heat.

Bill sat down next to Janice and Elizabeth. Both women were solemn after losing Kathy. He knew what they felt. Kathy had been a fun, positive woman, always full of smiles despite everything she'd experienced before reaching the school. And now she was dead.

Screams and yells caused him to stand up and walk over to the edge of the roof.

The front lawn of the school was filled with people from all walks of life. Janitors, lawyers, housewives and mechanics. Some wore clothing that made their professions easy to identify, but others wore torn, ripped and sometimes bloody clothes, their identities a mystery other than their sex. They staggered around, jumping and pushing each other.

"There's more of them," Bill said to no one in particular.

The outbreak happened so gradually that at first no one realized what was happening. The police chalked it up to a few psychotics, but then it continued to grow until the police couldn't contain all the outbreaks.

The news could only hypothesize about the origin of the psychosis. The words "terrorist" and "biological warfare" were tossed around until they meant nothing. But in the end all anyone had were guesses.

Outbreaks began to appear across the globe. Flights were canceled. Countries closed their borders. But they didn't close them fast enough: whatever the virus was, it had reached every corner of the world and was consuming people at an astounding rate.

Before Bill had abandoned his home, the percentage figures on the local news estimated that, by the same time next week, the entire world would be infected.

What the eggheads in Washington and across the world didn't realize was that a small portion of the population was immune to the sickness. Though Bill had never won anything his entire life and considered himself unlucky, he'd won the most important lottery ever to be played. So had all the others on the roof. Still, he wondered if the animals yelling and screaming below him were the lucky ones.

Bill looked across the treetops to the skyline of Chicago a few miles away. Where once tall buildings glittered with lights, fires burned in the darkness. Off to his right, the Sears Tower blazed like a beacon for approaching ships, the steel girders glowing white hot.

He sighed. He had no idea how they were supposed to survive what was happening to them, but he knew for a fact he wouldn't go down without a fight.

For now he decided to just rest. He'd earned it.

Janice offered him a lifeless smile as he sat down next to her again. Bill returned it and closed his eyes, trying just for a moment to ignore the sounds of the mad below.

CHAPTER 2

Bill opened his eyes to the sound of raised voices. On the opposite side of the roof, Becky and Mike were arguing.

He didn't know what the argument was about, but Mike was waving his arms around; it looked like it might come to blows at any second.

Some of the others were watching the couple, curious. Others could have cared less, thinking only of their problems and what they were going to do about them.

Bill rose to his feet. Marie came up to his side and nodded in the direction of Mike and Becky.

"They're having quite the disagreement, aren't they?" she asked with a wry smile.

"Seems so. As long as it's just words, I reckon it's none of our affair, but if it becomes physical ... well, that's where I draw the line."

Marie nodded. "Nothing to do but wait then."

"Guess so."

They stood together watching Mike and Becky. Bill had to admit the little spitfire gave as well as she got.

She took a step closer to Mike, so close she could probably smell his breath. That's when Mike pushed her away. She landed on her butt, the gravel cushioning her fall, her hands digging divots in the small pebbles.

Mike advanced on her, and that was when Bill decided to step in.

"Good luck," Marie said as he walked away from her.

"Thanks, I think I'll need it."

Becky climbed to her feet and sent a few choice curse words at Mike. He raised his hand as if to strike her, but Bill caught his arm.

"Why, you old bastard," Mike said. "Finally decided to try and get a piece of me? Well, here!" He spun, throwing a fist towards Bill's jaw.

The punch was sloppy, but Mike was a strong man and Bill saw stars for a few seconds. He backed away, shaking his head to clear it and rubbing his bruised jaw. He almost didn't see the next punch.

He dodged to the left; Mike's punch went wide.

Gritting his teeth, Bill decided the time for talk was over.

Like Marie had said, if the two men were ever going to co-exist, one of them would have to knock some sense into the other.

Bill brought his hands up in the classic boxer's stance, and Mike started to laugh.

"What the hell is this?"

Bill said nothing. He lashed out, fast and hard, and Mike doubled over, clutching his side. Sucking in gasps of air, he stood up and flexed his hands, ready to tear Bill apart. "That was a big mistake, old man."

Marie stepped closer, realizing someone could get hurt. "Both of you stop fighting this instant. We need to work together or we'll never get out of here."

Mike glanced at her. "Screw that, old woman. It's time to decide who's in charge once and for all." He lunged and wrapped his arms around Bill's waist, squeezing the breath out of him as he picked him up off the roof.

Bill tried desperately to suck in air, but Mike's arms were powerful from years of weightlifting, and Bill quickly realized he would never win a close-quarters brawl with the younger man.

He brought up both arms and slapped his palms against Mike's ears as if clapping a set of cymbals. Mike howled in rage, dropping Bill as he reached up to cup the sides of his head. He now heard a soft ringing he couldn't seem to shake.

Bill stepped away from him, sucking in great lungfuls of air. He was lightheaded, but with each breath his head began to clear.

By now all the other survivors had gathered around the two men. Some cheered for Bill while others seemed to root for Mike.

"Not bad, old man," Mike said. He brought his hands away from his ears and spit a wad of phlegm onto the roof. "But I promise you that will be your last shot."

Bill brought his fists in front of him again, this time determined to stay out of reach of Mike's massive arms. He cupped his hand, gesturing his opponent to have at it.

With a snarl, Mike charged forward and Bill danced aside. When Mike passed him, Bill landed a roundhouse blow to the back of his neck, directly over the spine.

Mike landed on the gravel of the roof like a baseball player sliding into first base. He quickly rolled over and climbed to his feet, although a little woozier than before he'd gone down.

Bill decided it was time to end this. He stepped close and sent two shots into Mike's midsection. The kid bent over from the blows, and Bill hit him with an uppercut right under the chin.

Mike's head flew back like he'd been shot, and he dropped to the roof. He was still moving, but not fast enough to defend himself.

Bill approached him slowly, not knowing what to expect. He leaned down on one knee and whispered into Mike's ear. "As far as I'm concerned, we're done, unless you want to keep going."

Mike's eyes were glazed with pain and he shook his head.

Bill stood up and wiped gravel from his knee. "Okay then, I guess this discussion is closed." He walked over to Becky, and Marie followed him.

"You okay?" Bill asked.

Becky nodded and looked down at her feet, close to tears.

"What were you two arguing about, dear?" Marie asked.

Becky looked past them to check on Mike. He had sat up, and despite a few bruises he seemed to be recovering nicely.

She looked back to Bill and shrugged. "Nothing really. Mike just said we should get out of here. You know, leave the school, maybe find a better place to go."

Bill's eyebrows went up in surprise. "Better? And just where would that be? Hell, if he knows something I don't ..."

Becky shook her head, her hair falling in front of her face. "That's just it. He doesn't know where to go; he just wants to leave. I said I wanted to stay here with you guys." Her voice grew soft. "That's when he pushed me and started to really get angry. It's my fault, though; I shouldn't have disagreed with him."

Marie and Bill looked at each other.

"Becky," Marie asked softly, "did Mike ever hit you before all this craziness started to happen to the city?"

Becky shrugged again. "No, not really. I mean, sometimes I do things to upset him. It's my fault really."

Bill placed a hand gently on her shoulder. "That's a load of bull, Becky, and you know it. No one should ever be hitting you, especially your boyfriend."

Mike stood and called out to Becky. "Hey, baby, I'm sorry about that. I was wrong." He extended his right hand to her.

Becky looked at Bill, then Marie. "He said he was sorry. Look, he's all I've got." She slid between them and walked over to Mike, who put an arm around her waist to keep her from moving away from him.

Bill watched them go. "Christ, with everything that's happening, now we've got a wife beater on our hands."

"Well, technically," Marie said, "he's not one. After all, they're not married."

"Jesus, Marie, he beats her like a sack of potatoes and you give me semantics?"

She smiled. "What else should I do? No matter how much we dislike the situation, it's still her choice. If she wants to stay with him, then good luck to her."

Bill threw up his hands. "The whole damn world is going nuts and I'm stuck with you and your damn rationalizations."

She patted his back and chuckled, and the two of them rejoined the others to explain the argument and the following fistfight.

On the other side of the roof, Mike sat down on the edge, letting his legs swing off the side. Becky plopped down next to him and stayed silent until she was spoken to.

Mike closed his eyes, trying to let the anger and frustration flow through him. The cool breeze calmed him and dried the perspiration covering his face and arms. He looked over his shoulder at Bill. Before, he'd just disliked the man, but now he wanted him dead—especially after being humiliated in front of Becky and the others.

The old man had fought pretty well, much better than Mike would have expected. But if Bill thought their feud was over, he was wrong. Dead wrong.

CHAPTER 3

Bill plopped down onto the roof, his body sore in places that had been just fine before the fight. His legs dangled over the edge, far above the screaming mob. He chuckled to himself. No matter how hard he tried to resist it, old Father Time would always remind him he wasn't twenty anymore.

He thought of his wife then, her beautiful face, her long brown hair. That was how he tried to remember her, full of life and beauty, not the withered husk of a dying woman.

She had fought valiantly for years, but once the chemotherapy failed she knew it was the end.

Bill had spent his last moments with her, sitting on the edge of the bed they had made love in countless times. When he'd looked into her eyes, it was like she knew her time was up. She had smiled wanly at him; even in the end she was stronger than he was. He would have given anything to take her place, to let her live for years to come, but God or whatever force that made the rules had deemed to take her instead.

Before she died, she told him not to give up on life, that he needed to keep on living for the both of them. She made him promise. But since her passing he'd been loath to meet another woman. He didn't want to desecrate her memory.

Now, as he sat on the edge of the roof and watched all the infected people wandering around below him, he realized if he made it through this—whatever *this* was—then he would follow through on his promise and start living again.

Marie finished filling the others in about the fight and walked over to Bill. He gestured for her to sit down next to him, and with a groan she plopped down and chuckled.

Bill smiled halfheartedly, not in a jovial mood, but Marie was just a natural at bringing out the good in people.

She noticed his smile and shot one back of her own, only three times as large as before. "What, do I amuse you?"

He nodded. "As a matter of fact, you do. Muscles a little sore?"

Her lips became a thin line. "Afraid so. Arthritis. How 'bout you?"

Bill shook his head. "No, I've been lucky so far. A few aches and pains in the morning, but nothing that slows me down."

"I saw. You handled yourself pretty well against Mike, and that boy must be half your age."

Bill shrugged. "Did some boxing back in college. Guess it's like riding a bike."

One of the crazies below threw a glass bottle at the school, trying to reach Bill and Marie. The bottle smashed against the red brickwork on the second floor. Shards of glass rained down on the crowd, and many of the psychos turned their faces away to avoid the debris. More howls of pain and madness filled the night.

Marie watched with mild interest. "You know," she said, "they are us and we are them."

Bill watched her face to see if she was going to elaborate, but she didn't. "Can't say I agree with you on that one, Marie.

Whatever the hell has happened to those people, I just thank God it hasn't happened to me." He looked down at the crowd. Even in the darkness he could see their faces, their eyes and teeth reflecting ambient light. The power was still on in the neighborhood and the streetlamps cast bright circles about the street.

"There are some things worse than death," Bill said softly.

Marie turned to look at him. His face was nothing but a shadow mixed in with the night. "Like what?" she asked.

He shrugged. "Like losing your own sense of identity, for one. Those people down there and all the rest—they're changed now. Whatever they once were—teachers, doctors, truck drivers—it's gone. Now all that's left is the instinct to hunt and kill. They don't even have their personalities, and without that we're nothing more than a bag of meat. Now maybe some scientist somewhere will figure out a way to reverse what's happened, but until they do, we are most definitely on our own."

"Okay," Marie said, "and what does all that mean for the rest of us?"

Bill turned to look at her, his face set in a hard grimace. "Well, for one thing, we need to get off this roof or we're going to die up here."

As if to illustrate his statement, a pack of crazies hollered up at them, their hands opening and closing as they imagined pulling Bill and Marie from their perch.

Marie felt a chill. And she hoped that chill was in no way some form of premonition. "But we're safe here, aren't we? I mean, if we go down there ... that would surely spell our doom."

Bill chuckled. "You make is sound like we're in a bad horror movie. But yeah, it's dangerous. Thing is, without food and water, and how hot the sun's been getting, we'll die anyway if we don't leave. And if we don't do it soon we'll be too weak to change our minds."

"I guess you're right," Marie said. "Well, I'm off to tell the others. Good night, Bill." She planted a hand on her knee and pushed herself up.

As Bill watched her go, he caught Mike staring at him from the other side of the roof. Bill shivered. For whatever reason he had made himself an enemy, and he knew when it was time to leave, he needed to keep Mike where he could see him.

The rest of the night was uneventful, and despite the shouting crowd of people surrounding the school, Bill finally managed to grab a few hours of fitful sleep. In his dreams, raging lunatics hounded him. Sometimes he escaped, and other times he went down under an avalanche of human bodies. Each time before they ripped the flesh from his body, he would wake up, his heart pounding in his chest.

After the last nightmare, he decided to stay awake. The sun was just starting to rise, sending its warm rays across the neighborhood.

Off in the distance, Chicago continued to burn. He wished for the hundredth time that someone at the school had a radio or a cell phone. He would give almost anything to know what was happening beyond the street the school was on.

Ever since they'd come to the school, they hadn't seen another non-infected person, only snarling, screaming animals that walked upright.

Could they be the only survivors in the entire Chicago area? It was a chilling thought.

Bill looked up when Melissa walked over and plopped down next to him. Her hair glowed like fire in the sun. Shaking her head so that the wind blew the bangs out of her face, she smiled at him. "Hey."

Bill smiled. "Hey, yourself." Though he was far from shy around women, he had to admit he was attracted to Melissa. He had no way of knowing if she felt the same, and with their dire situation he figured it wasn't the right time to ask.

"Marie filled us in ... about your idea to leave," she said.

"Good, that's good. So what do you think?"

She nodded. "I think you're right. We need to get out of here, and fast, before more of those people show up down there. So far, they're all in front of the school; it shouldn't be too hard to sneak away from the rear of the building. The only thing is ..." She hesitated and Bill picked up on her thoughts.

"The only thing is, where do we go from here?" he finished.

Her smile grew wider, her eyes glinting in the sunlight. "Exactly."

Bill frowned. "You know, I haven't thought that far ahead, but we need to decide quickly. Why don't you share with the others, see if anybody has ideas. Tell them no idea's too stupid, the more the better."

Her smile never wavered and she climbed to her feet, wiping gravel off her butt. "You got it." Melissa trotted off to the others, some of who were just waking up. Without food it would be easy to motivate them. Bill wanted to get off the roof as soon as possible so he could find something to eat. He was starving.

And he needed to take a piss. Standing on the edge of the roof, Bill emptied his bladder all over the crowd below. Angry cries floated up to him as the mass separated to avoid the stream. He swung to the left and right to get them, his urine arcing like a poor excuse for a waterfall.

Finished, he zipped up and turned away from the edge, surprised to see Marie standing behind him, crossing her arms like a stern matron. Her frown made her look just like his grandmother, made him feel like a small child caught eating cookies before dinner.

"Was that really necessary?" she asked.

Bill shrugged. "Probably not, but it felt good. It's not like they can get any madder at us than they already are. I mean, they want to kill us, right? So how exactly does my pissing on them make it any worse?"

She chuckled. "You know, that makes too much damn sense for me to argue with you." She changed the subject.

"Listen, everybody's awake and wants to talk about leaving. Evidently you aren't the only one who wants out of here. We're all tired and hungry, so if you're ready, come join us."

"Right behind you," he said.

"There's a problem, Bill," Elizabeth said. She had taken him aside from the rest of the group. "Some of the others don't want to wait for a plan; they want to leave now."

"Now? Just how the hell do they plan to do that?"

Elizabeth pointed to the roof hatch. "They think they can sneak into the school and go out the back door."

Bill shook his head. "That's crazy. The moment they step foot off the ladder they'll probably be overrun. Look, let me talk to them."

"Okay, they're over there. The bald guy and the four others with him." Elizabeth gestured with her chin at the small knot of people huddling together.

Bill nodded to Melissa and thanked her for the heads up, and then Marie joined him as he walked over to the small group.

The leader of the small group was around forty or so, with no hair and a high forehead. His dirty white t-shirt was too short to cover his beer belly.

Bill barely glanced at the others. They weren't the decision makers here.

"So I hear you want to leave?" Bill stated calmly. "You should know the moment you step off that ladder you'll probably be torn to pieces."

Baldie shrugged. "That's not the way I see it. There hasn't been any banging on that hatch for hours. Way I see it, they all left for better pickings."

Bill nodded. "Perhaps. Or maybe they're just waiting patiently for someone stupid enough to go back down there."

Baldie laughed. "That's ridiculous and you know it. They're nothing but animals. They can't reason like you and me. Anyone with a brain can see that just by watching them for a few minutes."

"Well," Bill muttered, turning to Marie, "they can't reason like me, anyway." She grinned, but only for a second. She didn't want to agitate the bald man or any of his compatriots. "But why do you have to try now?" she asked. "Wait a while; give us a chance to come up with another escape plan. Surely, one of us will figure a safer way off the roof."

Baldie shook his head and crossed his arms over his man-breasts. "No deal. Look, I've already decided, and these people all agree with me. Now unless you're going to try and stop us ..." He trailed off as he looked down at the .38 in Bill's waistband.

"No, I won't stop you," Bill said. "If you want to kill yourself, and these deluded people want to follow you, have at it."

The man's face softened a little and he turned to his followers. Their faces told him they were still behind him.

"All right then," Baldie said, turning back to Bill and Marie. "We'll be going now, before the sun's fully up. Figure we got at least another fifteen minutes."

Bill held out his hand. "Listen, friend, I think you're making a big mistake, but good luck just the same."

Baldie was a little surprised, but he shook with Bill anyway.

To Baldie's followers, Bill said, "It's not too late to back out, you know. You don't have to go with him. We'll find a way out of here. A safe way, I promise."

Heads swayed back and forth and mouths became slits, the others behind Baldie all saying no.

"We think you're the crazy ones for staying up here," a skinny man behind Baldie said. "You'll die up here without food and water."

"Yeah," someone else said, and everyone else nodded.

Bill threw up his hands in surrender. "Fine. I give up. I'm done." He walked away, but Marie stayed behind.

She smiled sweetly at them, holding her gaze on each person for just a moment. "Are you sure now? Is there no way to change your minds?"

No one answered her.

"Okay then. Good luck and Godspeed."

Baldie clapped his hands and rallied his small group. Marie walked over to Bill and he glanced at her, his face set in stone. "They're going to their deaths, you know."

"Uh-huh. But it's their lives and last time I checked, it was still a free country."

Bill sighed as he watched the group start to leave. He decided if they were going, then he should at least help with the hatch; that way if there were any problems, he could shut it before things got out of control.

Baldie was already pulling the metal bar from the top of the hatch, preparing to go down first. The man glanced at Bill, but Bill was done talking. If the damn fool wanted to die, then so be it.

Baldie opened the hatch slowly, the sweat already dripping off his large forehead. Nothing but silence greeted him from below. He flashed Bill a smile, and then he stepped into the hatch and disappeared into the darkness.

For a few heartbeats, no one moved, waiting for the worst. "See," Baldie finally called up, his voice echoing. "I told you it was safe. Come on down and let's get out of here!"

One at a time, the four others went through the hatch, each saying bye to the people staying behind.

The last one, a young man in his early twenties, stopped on the ladder and looked up Bill. "Don't worry. Once we find help we'll tell them about you, I promise." Then his head disappeared and Bill slammed the hatch, securing the metal bar once more.

He turned to the others gathered around him. "No one opens that," he said, pointing at the hatch. "No matter what. They made their bed, now they can lie in it. Promise me."

"But what if they need to come back up?" Janice asked. "Like we did?"

"It's too late. They made their decision," Bill told her. "Now, does everybody agree, or are we going to have to vote on it?" His eyes darted to Mike, who gazed back with a blank face, no objection. *Good*, Bill thought.

One at a time the people in his group mumbled their agreement, then everyone scattered to their favorite places on the roof. With no sounds coming from below, Bill wondered if Baldie had been right, that he and the others were the crazy ones for staying on the roof.

Deciding it was too late for regrets, he stretched out by a ventilation unit. He picked the side opposite the rising sun, hoping to steal a little shade. Closing his eyes, he sighed and tried to see if he could catch up on some of the sleep he'd lost the night before, thanks to way too many nightmares.

Bill's eyes shot open to the shouts of the others. He checked his watch. He had been asleep for a little more than half an hour. People were hovering over the hatch, and as Bill climbed to his feet, he saw that Mike was about to slide the bar out of the handle. As bill ran toward them, he started to hear the banging and screams coming from below.

With his eyes still blurry from sleep, he staggered over to the others. "What the hell's going on?"

Melissa was closest and she filled him in on the situation. "It just started, screams from inside the school and then pounding. Someone's begging us to open the hatch!"

"What are we supposed to do?" Elizabeth screamed. "Let them die down there?"

"I'm opening the hatch," Mike stated, preparing to do just that.

Bill whirled on him and pulled the .38 from his waistband. "You'll do no such thing, unless you want a bullet in the chest. Look, Mike, this is nothing between us, but if you open that hatch those killers will get up here and I don't have enough bullets to stop them all. So for the love of God, back off!"

Mike's face hardened and he looked into Bill's eyes, then into the muzzle of the .38, like he was weighing his options. All the while the banging and screaming and pleas for help continued.

Bill curled his finger around the trigger. "Don't test me, Mike. I don't want to, but I will if it means keeping the rest of us safe."

Becky scooted up to Mike and tried to pull him away. "Come on, honey, those people aren't worth it. They chose to go down there and they knew what would happen if they did."

Mike's face softened a little, and if Bill had to guess, he was using Becky to back out of the confrontation without losing face with the others. "All right, baby, I'll do it for you." He pointed to Bill. "You win this one, old man, but you've sentenced those people to death!"

Bill nodded. "Won't be the first time. God help me, it probably won't be the last. It's a different world now, Mike. Sometimes the decisions might seem cruel, but they have to be made. The sooner you realize that, the better off you'll be."

Mike flipped him off and walked away. Becky followed like a puppy.

"All right then," Bill said, surveying the others around him, "no one touches that hatch!"

No one said anything. The small group of survivors huddled around the hatch and listened to the sounds of carnage until it stopped abruptly, like a door being slammed. No screams, no pleadings, just silence.

Bill lowered the .38. "Okay then; that ends that."

He waited for more than an hour and finally decided it should be clear inside the school. He called Melissa over to help him. "I want to see for myself what I already know to be true, but I think the others need to know. If everyone doubts me every time I make a decision, then what will happen the next time I make one?"

"What do you want me to do?" Melissa asked.

Bill kicked the hatch with his foot. I want you to open that for me. Don't worry, I'll cover you in case there's any surprises, but I'm pretty sure it's safe now."

"Pretty sure? I don't know, Bill."

"Look, there's been nothing for more than an hour. Whatever was down there has moved on."

She sighed. "Fine, but you better have me covered; I don't feel like dying today."

He chuckled and waved for her to open the hatch. She slid the bar free and set it down in the gravel. Then, with her heart in her throat, she opened it, slowly at first, but when no hands shot out to grab her, she opened it all the way.

The sun, high overhead, shined directly into the opening. Marie and Elizabeth had joined Bill, and as one group they looked into the opening, their heads blocking out most of the light. The first thing they saw was the underside of the hatch. Before, it had been painted a dull gray color, but now partially dried blood coated the entire inside. Bits of gristle and meat hung from the ladder rungs and pools of blood covered the floor of the hallway. Bill quickly turned away, the smell of death too much to take.

"You can close it; I think I got my answer. Make sure you tell the others, too. They need to know. Hopefully after this, no one will do anything too foolhardy."

Melissa let the hatch fall shut and slid the bar back in place. Marie patted Bill's shoulder and walked away.

He'd been right all along and now five more of them were dead.

Looking out across the horizon, he wondered just how many more would lose their lives before their odyssey was finished.

CHAPTER 4

Dean Carlson smiled, feeling pretty good about himself. He sat in an abandoned coffee shop, his arms folded on the table in front of him, his chin resting on one of his arms. A pretty blonde was slumped unconscious in the chair across from him. He watched her ample cleavage rise and fall with each breath.

Dean was what people would call uninspired, though in fact he was really quite bright. He had barely graduated high school and had gone to work full time to survive, so college had been out of the question. Before Chicago had fallen apart from the inside out, he'd been a dishwasher for a small bistro on the edge of town. He had no parents. He was an orphan from the age of five.

His parents had gone out for a night on the town, and a drunk driver had jumped the median, killing them both. With no other close relatives, Dean found himself tossed into foster home after foster home until finally he turned eighteen. After that, he was given a pat on the back and a hearty good luck and was sent out into the big, wide world.

He'd floated from job to menial job until landing the dish-washing gig. It didn't pay much, but he got to eat all the left-overs he could stomach. Sometimes the owner would let him take food home to his one-room apartment situated in nothing more than a glorified boarding house. Up until a few days ago, the best Dean had to look forward to were a couple of leftover steaks or an extra bowl of soup. But now it seemed he'd been given a new destiny.

Unfortunately, he still didn't quite know what that destiny was.

The blonde's shirt had lost a few buttons and half of her left breast was trying to break free of her bra. If it had have been a few days ago he would have been aroused, but now it did nothing for him. In fact, the vein pulsing on the side of her throat seemed to stimulate him more than her bosom.

Suddenly, his pants felt too snug and he shifted in his chair to get comfortable. That was when the woman moaned and her eyes fluttered open.

"Oh, where am I?" she asked, her head snapping up and around as she tried to look every which way at once.

"We're in a coffee shop," Dean said. "You should be safe ... for now."

Sitting up, she pulled her shirt closed and tried to compose herself. Panic filled her eyes and she got ready to bolt out of the shop.

Dean held up his hands. "Whoa, I wouldn't do that if I were you. The second you run out that door they'll be on top of you, I guarantee it."

She blinked and began to settle down. "How did you get us here safely?" she asked, frowning. "I was being chased by a dozen or more of those lunatics. Why didn't they tear us apart?"

When Dean had first bumped into her, she'd been running from a large group of the Changed. She saw Dean and immedi-ately fell into his arms. "Help me," she whispered, "please," and then she passed out from fatigue. Dean had half-carried, half-dragged her into an abandoned coffee shop, where he'd set her in a chair and waited for her to recover.

"We're not lunatics," Dean told her politely. "We prefer to be called the Changed. Or at least I do."

The woman blinked again, as if seeing Dean for the first time. Sitting casually across from her was a slim, non-descript man with brown hair and rough skin. If she had to guess, he probably had an acne problem when he was younger. He was dressed in a long-sleeve button-down shirt and a pair of tan Dockers.

All in all, she saw nothing threatening about the man—after all, he had saved her—yet every time she looked into his eyes she got the creeps.

"How come they didn't attack you and me when I ran into you?" she asked. "We should both be ... dead."

Dean shrugged. "That's easy; I told them to leave us alone."

"And they do what you tell them? But how, why?"

Dean leaned closer to her and grinned, his teeth flashing in the wan light of the coffee shop, his eyes squinting malevolently. "That's easy. I'm one of them. I don't know why, but they listen to me. Pretty cool, huh? I can tell them to do whatever I want, though I haven't thought about what to do with them yet. So far I've just had them get me food and clothes."

The woman slid off her chair and started backing up toward the front door. Dean just sat in his chair, grinning.

Her footsteps made crackling sounds as she stepped over the broken glass carpeting the floor. For the first time since waking, she realized the coffee shop was a shambles. It seemed not a single cup or dish had been spared. Mirrors had once lined one wall to make the shop appear bigger, but now every mirror was shattered, the silver pieces reflecting the dim light filtering in from the street.

When the blonde reached the front door, she allowed herself a sigh of relief. Evidently, Dean meant her no harm; he was still seated. She turned for the door, but stopped as if she'd walked into an invisible barrier. Outside in the street, amidst the abandoned cars and taxicabs, were dozens, if not hundreds, of lunatics.

Everyone she could see was covered in red and scarlet. She knew it had to be blood.

But their eyes were the most disconcerting. Despite that the crowd moved like a pack of animals, their eyes were glazed over, as if they were staring at something far away for all eternity—until they turned to her and their mouths curved into feral grins; their teeth flashed in the sunlight, their lips tinted red from fresh kills. She wouldn't be leaving that way anytime soon.

She heard footsteps behind her and turned. Dean, not more than a foot behind her, grabbed her by the throat and pushed her against the wall. She struggled, unable to understand how this skinny man, about the same size as her, could pin her so forcefully against the wall. He had almost lifted her off the floor.

"Don't," she croaked, barely able to speak.

He laughed at her. "Don't? Why not? I can do anything I want to. And there's literally no one to stop me."

Dean snapped her neck like a dry twig. He supposed he should have tortured her more, but he found he liked the dramatic snap of her neck; it had felt right.

He dragged the corpse to the front door and tossed it into the street. Immediately, the Changed surrounded her and started to rip the pretty blonde corpse to pieces.

Dean looked away, disinterested.

So he hadn't tortured her; that was okay. He'd just make up for it on the next normal he came across.

While the Changed fed on the woman in the street, Dean went back inside and walked behind the counter.

After smelling all the rich Columbian beans, he realized he was dying for a cup of coffee.

CHAPTER 5

Bill gazed down at the murderous mass below him. The bodies seemed to ebb and flow like the tide. Every so often two of the crazies would turn on one another, and a fight would break out. The fight wouldn't stop until one of the opponents lay dead in the dirt, bleeding out onto the crushed grass that lined the front of the school.

Leaving the screams of the crowd behind him, Bill walked away from the edge. The others stood in the center of the roof, talking amongst themselves and looking as tired and scared as he felt.

Near the back of the group, Roger and Phillip stood quietly, their young faces almost blank. The two boys had been through a lot, and if Bill was right, there would be more hell to come before they were safe. Mike and Becky were there too, keeping to the outside of the circle.

When he was only a few feet away, Melissa moved closer to him, slowing him before he reached the others.

"We've been talking and we've all decided it's time to get off this roof. We're all hungry and thirsty and with the sun up it's only going to get worse."

Elizabeth stepped forward. "That's right, we all want to go."

Janice stood next to her, arms folded. The light wind blew her across her face, no matter how many times she brushed it back.

Before he said anything to the others, Bill looked to Marie for advice. The woman had become a good sounding board for his conscience, like a big sister.

"All right now," Marie said, walking over to Bill, "just everyone calm down. Nothing has been decided yet. Before we leave here, we need to have a plan of action. We need to know where we're going once we leave, or we won't get twenty feet before we're attacked."

"You mean we need a distraction so we can get away from them, right?" Janice asked. Everyone looked at her, and she started to backpedal. "I mean ..."

Bill nodded and grinned. "You're right," he said, running with the idea. "We need a way to keep those bastards down there at the front of the school, so we can climb down the other side and disappear into one of the back yards across the street."

The school was situated in the middle of more than a dozen suburban streets, all with neat rows of middle-class homes. The houses all appeared to be abandoned.

If they were lucky, they could run through a backyard and out to one of the side streets. From there they could find transportation or hide out in one of the many houses, maybe one of the basements or attics.

True, it might not have been the best plan, but so far it was all he had.

"How the hell are we gonna get down from here?" Mike asked, his voice cold and low. "It's not like you have a ladder up your ass that you can pull out for us to use."

"That's true, Mike," Bill said, deciding to answer him, whether or not his question was rhetorical. "I've been thinking about that, too. What about if we all take off a piece of clothing and tie it together to make a half-ass rope? I mean, if we make sure the knots are tight enough, we should be able to get down all right."

People turned to look at each other and voices rose as the group discussed the idea.

"Even if we did that and we all ran around in our underwear, that still doesn't explain how the heck we're going to distract those nutjobs long enough to get away from here," Melissa pointed out.

That started more voices and arguments. Marie stood next to Bill, watching the group with a sly grin on her face. Bill noticed this and leaned in close so only she could hear him.

"You look like the cat that's eaten the canary," he said. "What's so amusing?"

She shrugged. "Nothing really. It's just this is the first *real* time that they're all listening to you. It seems your disagreement with the bald man and his friends did more to elevate your status as leader than anything else you've done."

He frowned. "You know, I never asked to be in charge of anything. I'm no better than anyone else around here."

"That's right, Bill, and that's why you're perfect for the job." She stepped away from him and held up her hands to quiet the others. Bill stood silent, not quite understanding what she meant. He decided if they had a chance later, he would ask her to explain, but for now he had a meeting to finish.

When Marie had everyone quiet, all of them eager to hear what their leader had to say next—with the exception of Mike, who stood with his arms crossed—Bill cleared his throat and stepped into the middle of the group.

"All right, look, I'm no leader, but if you'll let me, I'll give it a try. This means that, with the exception of something we put to a vote, you have to listen to what I tell you." He held up his hand when some of the others prepared to say something.

"Now before you answer me, let me explain. If we need to do something quick out there or hide or whatever, I need to know that you'll do it and not start arguing about it every time. There's a reason why on a battlefield there's only one man in charge, and this is pretty damn similar. If you don't want me to lead, that's fine, but I tell you what: if we don't make someone the leader soon, then most of us will never make it out of here. We need to stick together and fight; it's the only way we're going to make it alive and in one piece."

Finished, he waited for their answer. If what Marie said was true, then they would agree with him. If not, well, that was fine with him. Let someone else deal with the responsibilities.

It was Melissa who stepped forward first. She pulled Bill a few feet away from the group, then turned to face them. With her head held high and a fire in her eyes to match her red hair, she said, "He's right. We need a leader, and I say Bill's the one for the job. Who's with me?"

Marie came next, followed by Elizabeth and Janice. Janice held out her hand to the two boys and they walked over to join Bill's supporters.

That left Becky and Mike. For a brief moment everyone was quiet, except for the crazies howling below.

"Well, Mike," Marie said, "what do you say?"

"Don't see as I've got any goddamn choice in the matter," Mike said, staring at Bill.

Becky squeezed his arm slightly and placed her head on his shoulder. "Aww, come on, honey, don't be like that. Forgive and forget, please?"

Mike sighed. "Fine, whatever," he said with a wave of his arms. "He's in charge." He walked away, leaving Becky alone in front of the rest of the group.

She smiled at Marie and Bill. "See, I told you he's not that bad of a person." Then she ran off across the roof to catch up to her boyfriend.

"All right then, meetings over for now," Bill said. "Everyone think of a way to make a distraction and get back to me or

Marie. The sooner the better, people." He clapped his hands, shooing them to different parts of the roof.

Once everyone was dispersed in groups of twos and threes, talking animatedly amongst themselves, Bill looked to Marie. "Well, there you have it. The first meeting of Survivors Anonymous. All in all, I think it went well."

She chuckled. "Suppose so. After what happened with Mike last night, anytime you two don't get into a fight, I'll call it a success."

"Very funny, you're a riot. You know, you should take that act on the road; you'd be rich. Hell, I bet the *Tonight Show* would even book you."

The two of them walked toward the rear of the roof to check the area one more time before deciding on a course of action. As they walked, Marie slipped her arm in Bill's and winked at him slyly.

"You joke, but when this is all over I may do just that, just to prove you right."

He shook his head and laughed a little. Though they were in dire peril and their chances for survival were slim, he still felt the need to laugh, no matter how trivial the reason. Because if he didn't laugh, he'd probably just start crying.

CHAPTER 6

Bill checked his wristwatch for the fifth time in as many minutes. Looking up at the blazing sun high overhead, he squinted and shielded his eyes with his hand. It was going on noon and they still had not come up with a reasonable distraction to get them safely off the roof.

Despite this, the survivors had each donated a piece of clothing to make a rope. Most of the women now were without shirts, their white bras a weird contrast to their otherwise clothed bodies. Bill, too, was minus his shirt, and his white t-shirt was already wet with perspiration.

His mouth felt like sandpaper and he believed he would have given the next twenty years of his life for just one glass of water. Watching the faces of the others, he could see they were all feeling the same.

Marie walked up to him, and despite that she was more than ten years his senior, he couldn't help but notice that her breasts still appeared firm inside her white under-wire bra; her waist was still slim, only the barest amount of extra fat exposed above her waistband.

Realizing he was staring, he quickly turned his gaze to look at something else. A tree, one of many, grew across the street from the school, the branches full of leaves, waving in the wind. That seemed as good a place as any to concentrate his gaze.

Marie stopped next to him and looked out over the roof, same as him. Bill knew she was there, but hoping she hadn't seen him staring at her chest, he decided to play stupid.

"So, you like my tits, do you?" she asked. "I guess I owe you a thank you, especially with all the younger women bouncing around up here."

Bill's jaw dropped so low he thought he might kick it with his foot accidentally. "Excuse me?"

"I'm just messing with you, Bill, don't worry." She chuckled. "You should see your face; you look like a teenager who's just seen his girlfriend naked for the first time ... priceless."

"I'm sorry if I offended you, it's just ..." He debated how to say it, so he just said it. "It's just you look pretty good without your shirt on. I never would have guessed you had that kind of figure under your clothes."

She shrugged. "Well, now you know. I never got into wearing sexy outfits. Always wore things that weren't very flattering. Guess that's why I never landed a man."

Bill moved around a few pieces of gravel with his foot, feeling very uncomfortable with the conversation, especially with her standing there in nothing but her bra.

Luckily, Marie changed the subject. "So, I've talked with the others and no one has come up with a way to distract those lunatics long enough for us to leave. How about you? Anything come to mind?"

Shaking his head, he kicked away the piece of gravel he'd been toying with. The small stone rolled off the edge of the roof and dropped into the crowd below. The stone struck a man on the forehead and he let out a savage scream that was lost with the roar of the mob.

"I got nothing, but I'll tell you this, whether we come up with something or not, we need to go soon. Are you as thirsty as I am?"

She nodded, wiping her brow with the back of her hand. The sun was hot on their heads, and the heat even reflected off the roof itself; it had to be over ninety.

"Thirstier," Marie said. "I'd give my left boob for a drink right now."

Bill opened his mouth again, shocked. "Marie, where's all this coming from?"

She sighed. "I'm sorry, Bill, I'm just tired, and when I get tired I get a little loopy. Just ignore me; once we get out of here, I'll be okay."

Bill grunted, then looked beyond her to see the group finishing the makeshift rope. Melissa and Janice pulled on it, testing to see whether the knots would unravel when the first person tried to climb down.

As Melissa tugged on one of the last shirts the knot unraveled, and she fell to the hot rooftop in a spray of gravel. An instant later, she was back on her feet, brushing the hot stones from her skin. From where Bill stood, he could see small red dots on her back where the rocks had burned her. Otherwise, she appeared to be fine.

She saw him looking and waved to him, signaling that she was fine. Then she and Janice went back to testing the rope.

"She's a tough one," Marie said.

Bill looked at Marie. "Who, Melissa? Yeah, I guess so; she seems to be able to keep a level head. Smart, too."

"That she is. If we need someone to help with keeping the others in line, she's the one to ask," Marie said.

"Well, I just hope it doesn't come to that. Besides, once we're out of here, I wonder how many of us will just go their own way?"

Marie crossed her arms. "Why do you say that? You don't think we'll all stay together once we're down from here?"

"That's right, you just watch. Once we're away from here, everybody will have their own ideas of what we should do. We'll break apart quicker than a cardboard boat in the middle of the ocean."

"You might be right, but I guess it won't really matter until we're down, and if we can't find a distraction to keep those bastards from the rear of the school, then it won't matter at all. They'll be on us the second our feet touch the ground."

Bill grunted, a low sound in his throat that Marie barely heard. "Then I guess we better come up with one."

Two more hours passed, and still no one had thought of a suitable decoy. Bill was really starting to give up hope when a rumbling sound, followed by the sound of gunfire, caught his attention.

Running to the front of the school, followed by the others, he looked through the waving trees at the end of the street.

At first, he couldn't see anything, but as the rumbling and sounds of gunshots grew louder, the front bumper of a green and brown military truck pulled into view.

The murderous crowd below quickly moved off toward the new target.

"Oh my God, it's the Army," Elizabeth said. "They're coming to save us!"

Mike chuffed. "About damn time. They should have been here days ago back when all this shit started."

The staccato of gunfire filled the street, M-16s shooting at every target the soldiers could find. But as they moved closer, Bill quickly realized their salvation might not be coming as soon as they had hoped.

Squinting in the sun, he could see the truck had less than five men inside, at least two in the front cab, all wearing white biohazard suits. When they moved closer to the school, one of the men removed a tarp from the rear bed and exposed what looked like an M-60 machine gun. A soldier, no older than eighteen if he was a day, jumped behind the weapon and prepared it for battle. Another soldier, who looked only slightly older, had his back to the machine gunner, trying to keep the ever-growing crowd of attackers off his back.

The soldier sent the first rounds over the heads of the raving crowd, as if only trying to control them, warn them off, not destroy them. But when none of the raging killers seemed to care, he lowered the barrel of the weapon and fired into the attacking mob.

Bodies danced a macabre jig as bullets ripped into flesh and exploded organs. The street ran red with blood and blasted body parts as the soldier continued firing. But then, just as suddenly as the weapon had started firing, it stopped. The area around the school seemed preternaturally quiet after the deafening sound of the machine gun.

The soldier tried to un-jam the weapon, but bodies swarmed the truck, and soon the soldiers were outnumbered. The men retreated to the middle of the truck bed where they tried to hold off the murderous horde.

Bill watched for another instant and then snapped out of his trance. His heart, too, was filled with a false hope that was now quickly dashed away. But despite this, he saw one bright star in the darkness.

He saw the distraction they so sorely needed.

"Marie," he said, "we've got to go now, while those soldiers are keeping the crowd busy."

"Now? But we're not ready yet."

"Yes, right now, this second. Those soldiers are dead, and in less than a minute they'll be overwhelmed. But until then they're the distraction we need."

Marie looked at the truck and then back to him, then at the truck again, as if she couldn't comprehend what he was saying. But then her eyes went wide with understanding.

She looked at some of the others who were listening intently to the conversation, and then she nodded. "Bill's right. If we want to get off this roof alive, this is probably our best chance."

"All right then, what are we waiting for?" Melissa asked. "Let's get going." She slapped her hands together for emphasis.

Melissa, Bill and Marie herded the others away from the edge of the roof, while Mike hung back to watch the truck. Becky had left his side, and after a moment she realized he wasn't with her. She stopped and ran back to him.

"Come on, Mike," she said, grabbing his arm, "we have to leave. We don't want to be last."

Mike held his hand up to make her stop. "Quit it, Becky, I want to see what happens to the jarheads. They are so screwed."

Mike was right. The crowd of screaming killers finally overwhelmed the last soldier. He pulled his sidearm and fired point-blank into the closest attackers, but there were always two more to take the fallen killer's place.

They pulled the man from the truck and smashed him to the street, his white suit turning red. A mass of swirling bodies consumed him, each crazy vying for a piece, his cries soon buried under the shrieks of the beastlike crowd.

The truck's driver had been pulled from behind the wheel and the vehicle drove onward, still in gear. One of the psychos jumped inside and tried to steer it, but the man couldn't seem to comprehend the controls. The truck swerved and struck a tree, the motor still idling.

Becky pulled on his arm again and pointed to the rear of the school where Bill and Marie were going over the side.

"Come on, Mike, everyone's gone. We need to go."

Mike finally looked away from the truck; the show was over.

"Shit," he said, "they left us. Come on, Becky, what the hell are you waiting for? We have to leave."

She sighed, frustrated. "That's what I've been trying to tell you."

At the other side of the roof, Mike looked down just as Marie ran under a thicket of tree branches. The rest of the group was far from sight.

Sliding over the edge, he let his feet dangle for a moment until he knew he had a firm grip on the rope, then he started to shimmy down it, one foot at a time. He was young and strong and was on the street in seconds. He looked up to see Becky's head as she peeked down at him.

"Come on, damn it, what are you waiting for?" he yelled and whispered at the same time.

"I'm scared. I've always been scared of heights. You know that."

Mike expected a crowd of raving lunatics to run around the corner at any second and overwhelm him, but so far all was quiet at the rear of the school.

"Look," he said, "if you don't get your ass down here now, I'm leaving you up there!"

That seemed to be enough motivation for her, and she carefully swung her right leg over the edge. She winced as the heat of the roof burned her hands, and she slowly swung her body over the rest of the way. She reached out for the rope, which was tied to a pipe vent sticking out of the rooftop.

She started down slowly, much too slow for Mike's taste. She almost slipped, her hands losing grip. She screamed, managed to get a firmer grip. It didn't matter though. Her scream had echoed.

Mike cursed under his breath, knowing what was coming, but praying he was wrong.

Becky had made it almost halfway down when the first attacker came around the corner, his shoulder brushing the manicured shrubs that lined the school on all four sides.

The killer let out a piercing yell, signaling to the others he'd found more prey. Mike could only watch as more people, now soaked in the soldiers' blood, ran and hopped into view.

"Keep coming, Becky, you're doing fine," Mike called to her.

Her pants caught on a jagged piece of metal sticking out from the bricks, some kind of old hook or broken eyebolt. She slammed to a halt and looked over her shoulder to see the crowd of screaming people bearing down on them. Her arms were too tired; she couldn't pull herself up enough to unhook her pants.

"Mike, help me, I'm stuck."

"Damn it, Becky, there's no time. They're coming. We've got to go!" He had only seconds before he would be overrun and Becky, too.

"I can't, I'm stuck. You've got to climb up here and help me, please!"

Mike looked up at her and then at the crowd, then back to Becky. He wanted to help her, but if he wanted to live, he needed to leave. Hopefully Becky would distract them long enough for him to escape. "Sorry, baby, but you're on your own."

He took off at a run. Whether he was moving in the same direction as Bill and the others was irrelevant. All he knew was he needed to go now before they were on top of him.

Some of the crowd hesitated, deciding whether they wanted to chase him, but when Becky let out a howl of loss, they all focused on her.

"Mike, where are you going? Don't leave me, Mike!" She screamed as the first killer started to climb up the rope to reach her dangling foot and pull her to the ground.

Mike sprinted across the street, glancing over his shoulder to check on Becky. He regretted leaving her; she'd been a nice piece of ass and had done whatever he wanted. He'd totally controlled her. But that was all right, he thought as he darted into a perfectly manicured backyard. There were plenty more women in the world.

He turned to check on her one last time.

The ravenous crowd had reached the makeshift rope and was even now climbing up it. Becky hung on for her life as a growling, snarling, blood-covered man swung back and forth on her foot.

Just before Mike disappeared into the hedges of the yard, he saw her kicking at her first attacker, but she was hopelessly outnumbered and was soon pulled from the rope, her pants ripping free of the metal as she fell into the ravenous crowd. Her screams followed him for longer than he would have preferred.

CHAPTER 7

Bill caught up to the last person in their ragtag line, the man with the picture of his wife. Jogging alongside him, Bill tried to smile.

"Hey, I'm Bill, we were never introduced," he said in an upbeat, though breathless, voice.

"Bruce, Bruce Greenwood," the man said, his voice only wavering slightly from exertion.

"Nice to meet you, Bruce. I'd shake your hand, but I think it's better if we keep moving."

Bruce didn't answer. He slipped through an opening in a thicket of shrubs and slowed to a stop near the others, who had gathered in someone's backyard. Bill moved past him to Marie. Everyone was bent over or lying on the ground, trying to catch their breath. Whoever had been in the lead had picked a winding trail between multiple yards, and in no time they had run three blocks.

Bill bent over and placed his hands on his knees, sucking in another gulp of air. He smirked. Evidently his group wasn't in the best of shape. He closed his eyes, and the white spots slowly diminished as oxygen flooded his system.

"Looks like we lost them," Elizabeth said, one of the first to recover.

The savage screams of the crowd had diminished and could barely be heard. For just a second Bill thought he heard Becky scream, but he dismissed it as his imagination. On a normal day in the small town, background noise would have easily drowned out the sounds from the school, but with the streets literally empty except for the infected, sound traveled farther.

"So what's next? Where do we go from here?" Janice asked, lying on her back in the soft grass.

Marie said, "That's a good question, dear. Where is a safe place to go? Should we keep running or should we seek refuge in one of these houses?"

Bill had regained most of his composure, and he stood taller, looking over the survivors. They were missing someone.

"Hey, where's Mike and Becky?" he asked.

"Couldn't tell you," Elizabeth replied. "He was still on the roof when I climbed down." She wiped sweat from her brow. Perspiration glistened on her chest, making her skin glow.

Bill averted his eyes, not wanting to get caught looking at a woman's breasts twice in one day. He turned and jogged back to the opening in the shrubs. No one was following them, and it would be too dangerous to go after Becky and Mike. Had he heard Becky after all?

He double-checked to make sure the .38 was still tucked in the waistband of his pants and breathed a sigh of relief when he felt the weapon's comforting grip. It would have been too dangerous to go searching for it.

Walking back to the others, he frowned. "I could have sworn they were right behind me. Well, it's no use now; we can only hope they just chose to go their own way."

"All right then," Melissa said, stretching her legs as she cooled down from their brisk run. "That still leaves the question. Just where do we go from here?"

Bill was about to answer her when a loud rumbling filled the air. Everyone glanced around the yard as the sound grew louder.

"What the hell is that?" Janice asked.

"A train?" Melissa suggested.

Marie shook her head. "Can't be. The tracks are miles from here."

Bill looked up and to the left and saw a white shape falling toward them. Above the group, losing altitude fast, was a large passenger airplane. He wasn't a connoisseur of aircraft, but if he had to guess, he would have figured it was a 747 or something just as large.

The airport was miles away, and if a plane was cruising that low, it could only mean one thing.

"Holy shit," Bill screamed over the roaring engines, "that plane's coming down! We need to get the hell out of here—now!"

The people lying on the grass rolled to their feet again. The two boys, Roger and Phillip, huddled around Melissa and Janice, who hugged them close.

"What're you talking about?" Marie asked, looking at the descending airplane.

Bill grabbed her by the arm and pushed her out of the yard. "There's no time to discuss it. If you want to live past the next ten minutes, I suggest you all shut up and do what I tell you."

Everyone was looking at him, waiting, still not comprehending what he'd said.

"Listen, I was right when those people went down into the school and I'm right now, so do what I say!"

For a moment everyone hesitated, not grasping the situation.

"Did you hear me? I said run!" He bolted out of the yard and into the street, pulling his weapon out of his pants in case he met resistance.

The others filed out of the yard and followed him. Bill looked over his shoulder; the plane was getting closer with every beat of his heart. As he ran, a small voice told him to forget it; there was no way he could outrun a falling airplane.

He shoved the voice down as deep as it would go and pushed his legs to run faster. The others spread out behind him, running at their individual pace. Both Janice and Elizabeth actually passed him, but not so far that they couldn't see him and follow his lead.

Bill glanced over his shoulder to see the small boy Phillip falling behind. Cursing his luck, he refused to let him be run down and slaughtered like Walter and Kathy.

He stopped, waved the others forward, and scooped up the boy. Phillip wrapped his arms around Bill's neck. The boy barely weighed anything, no doubt because he had starved for a few days.

Pouring on the speed, Bill felt his teeth vibrating from the whining engines of the plane. He risked another glance over his shoulder—there was no way in hell they could outrun the falling aircraft.

As they ran down the street, numerous cars sat either in the road or halfway over the curb.

Spotting a Toyota van idling on the sidewalk, its front bumper wedged against a telephone pole, Bill ran over and jumped into the passenger seat. He ignored the blood on the steering wheel and dashboard, letting Phillip crawl into the back seat.

Bill put it in reverse and backed away from the telephone pole, wincing as the metal bumper shrieked and was torn off. Once he cleared the pole, he slammed the transmission in drive and shot forward, catching up to the others, still running down the road, in seconds. The side panels of the van were open, the wind whistling in his ears.

"Get in, now!" he screamed over the deafening noise. "It's the only way we'll outrun what's coming!"

While some of the group couldn't hear him, they figured out what he wanted them to do; with the van still rolling, they jumped inside one at a time. It was crowded in the van, far too many people for the small seats, but they managed to squeeze in.

Just as Bill was ready to floor it, a dozen men and women ran around the corner at the intersection. They saw the van but barely paid attention. They held their hands to their ears and some of them pointed at the descending plane.

Bill never hesitated. Just by their clothes and the way the crowd moved, he knew they weren't normal. He accelerated and plowed through them, bodies sprawling left and right.

A moment later he was through the throng, darting in and out of abandoned vehicles. He drove up onto the sidewalk, onto the lawns. Mailboxes and trashcans bounced off the windshield, bounced off the hood.

"Shit," Bill said. The needle on the gas gauge hovered over empty. And in the rearview, he could see the plane falling closer and closer, seconds away from striking the earth.

Going for broke, he floored the gas, and the van surged forward, driving over sixty down the sidewalk. The steering wheel constantly jerked side to side, and he jumped in his seat when an errant mailbox hit the windshield, sending a spider web of cracks across the safety glass.

Bill stuck his head out the window so he could see, and almost bashed his skull when he drove too close to a telephone pole.

The van felt like it was shaking apart as the rumbling turbines of the plane rose in pitch. Bill swerved around a car that had jumped the curb and shot down a side street.

He kept expecting the road to be blocked, the sidewalk and street choked with cars, but his luck held.

And then the plane hit.

Though he was ready for it, he never could have expected the magnitude of the explosion that ripped across the small neighborhood. The plane landed on top of nearly half a dozen homes, plowing through each one as it slid across the earth, never slowing.

The plane's fuel tanks belched out a fireball that consumed the entire block, but when one of the gas lines under the street was punctured, true Hell on Earth began.

Louder than mortar rounds, the street behind the van erupted, foot after foot, block after block.

Bill veered around a stalled truck and tried to concentrate on moving forward, but brief glances in his side mirror told him he didn't have much chance.

Behind him, a massive fireball swelled two stories tall, the street exploding outward as if the demons of Hell had finally broken through the dimensions.

"Oh my God, Bill, we are so fucked," Marie said behind him. He was so flustered he didn't realize she'd cursed.

A small picture of a gas pump lit up next to the gas gauge. Bill cursed. The van had idled for days on the sidewalk, perhaps starting out with a full tank; now only fumes were left.

All he could do was pray to God, Buddha or Allah—at the moment he would take help from any one of them.

The column of fire nipped at the rear of the van, and Bill started sweating, either from nerves or the rise in temperature. His passengers were screaming, and some were crying as they watched the inferno grow closer.

Tires screeching around a sharp corner, Bill plowed into a woman who tried to jump on the van. He saw her eyes, wide with rage, for the briefest instant before she was thrown off the hood. He looked in his rearview mirror, and the woman stood up, cut and bruised. She raised her hands in front of her face, as if that could protect her, and was quickly consumed by the wall of fire.

Bill looked forward, swerving, weaving. He had no way of knowing how far he'd traveled or how much farther he needed to go before they escaped the roaring conflagration.

As he steered around a few bodies lying on the sidewalk, he was amazed he and his friends weren't incinerated yet. He probably wouldn't feel a thing, the flames consuming him in an instant, his eyes melting, his skin flaking off his bones as it became nothing but charred ash.

Shaking drops of sweat off his brow and blinking hard to clear his vision, Bill let out a yell of elation when the road opened onto a highway, no cars in sight, the road clear. Thanking whatever deity had sent him this way, he turned up the onramp and floored the pedal yet again. The Toyota surged forward, and Bill squeezed the steering wheel to control the bouncing tires.

The fireball began to recede, but Bill kept going as fast as the van would let him. After the first quarter mile, the engine started chugging, and then it suddenly died. Fighting the brakes, which weren't cooperating with the engine off, he steered the van to the side of the road and finally stopped it.

He got out of the vehicle and opened the sliding passenger door. One at a time the others stepped out. They breathed shallowly through their mouths, trying not to cough on the smoke of burning homes and the high-octane smell of jet fuel.

Where there was once a neighborhood, now there was nothing but a giant crater, miles long. The underground gas pipes had continued to explode, one after another, street after street, until there was nothing left but flames.

Marie walked up to Bill on the shoulder of the highway, her feet crunching in the loose gravel and sand. He was surprised he could hear her footsteps over the roaring flames and secondary explosions.

"You saved us, Bill. I don't know how you knew it, but you did. If you hadn't thought quick and got us moving, we'd all still be in there." She stood on her tiptoes and kissed him on the cheek. "Thank you. From all of us."

Bill touched his cheek. "Thanks, I guess, but I just got lucky. If I hadn't found this van, we would have been toast. Literally."

She smiled. "Maybe. But you did find it and you did save us." She turned as the others walked up behind Bill. Bruce slapped him on the back, his face cheerful for the first time in days.

One at a time the others hugged him, their sweaty bodies sticking to his mostly bare chest, his t-shirt hanging ripped from sometime during their escape. The heat from the massive fire blew toward him, causing him to wince.

He said, "Come on, everyone. We need to go. The fire will keep on spreading until there's nothing left to burn, and I don't want to be around when that happens."

One at a time they set off up the highway, exhausted but cheerful. Each step they took and each lungful of air they breathed was a gift.

If any of them had questioned Bill's ability to lead them, all doubt had been swept away, like the pillars of smoke caught in the wind.

CHAPTER 8

Dean looked up from the man he'd been torturing on the ground. Off in the distance, at least five or six miles east, a huge explosion rocked the city. At first he thought it was an earthquake, though given the city's geology it would have been unlikely. Then he saw the giant fireball rising into the sky and realized it was just more wonderful chaos.

Evidently, something had happened in one of the suburbs surrounding Chicago.

Dean climbed off the *normal* lying in the street, now dead. He'd rumpled his clothes while killing the man. Quickly he tucked his shirt in and straightened his shirt sleeves. Just because he was a homicidal maniac didn't mean he couldn't look good.

Looking down at the body of the normal, its arms and legs bent at unnatural angles, Dean got an idea.

With the fire burning, any normal that had survived the blast would be evacuating the suburbs in search of a safe haven.

His mouth curved into an evil grin.

Why try to chase down every normal in the city? Instead, he could set the west end ablaze and let the fire flush them out.

Clasping his hands and rubbing them quickly with excitement, he got control of himself. Sometimes it was hard to stay focused. He always felt the rage inside him, threatening to come up from deep down in his mind and take over, threatening to turn him into something mindless like the other Changed surrounding him.

Only through sheer willpower had he managed to stay Dean Carlson.

He headed off to the edge of the city, gathering recruits as he went. He wasn't quite sure how he would get the deed done, but he'd always been a resourceful man. If everything went well, the city would be ablaze by sunset and every normal left alive would be running to him, like lemmings over the fabled cliff.

Mike, too, had seen the airplane falling out of the sky. When Bill and the others had run to the north, Mike had turned south.

With the roaring of turbines filling his head, he had found a useable motorcycle lying in the street. The small 200cc Kawasaki engine was more than enough to help him escape the growing fireball that swept through the quiet neighborhood behind him.

With the heat roasting his back and singeing his shirt, he'd raced through the debris-strewn streets until he came upon a roadblock. Military Hummers and large open-bed trucks blocked the street and the sidewalks on both sides, preventing Mike from passing. The personnel was nowhere in sight, although many maroon bloodstains covered the asphalt and the sides of the trucks.

Mike abandoned the motorcycle. He slipped through the barricade and darted into a two-story house bordering the road, heedless of what was inside. In the kitchen, he found the door to the basement. He threw it open and half-ran, half-fell down the rickety wooden stairs.

A workbench was in the corner, and he dove under it, covering his head with his hands as the world around him exploded. The shockwave of the plane crash blew the military barricade away and nearly disintegrated the house above him. It was like the mother of all hurricanes.

He screamed as the first floor of the house fell into the basement, dust and debris flying everywhere and filling every crevice.

Mike curled into a ball and prayed like he'd never prayed before, hoping God would answer his prayer this one time.

What seemed like hours passed, and the storm subsided. Everything became preternaturally quiet.

Mike pushed away a large wooden beam that had fallen over the sturdy workbench, which had saved him from being crushed. Coughing and spitting out dust, he started to dig himself out of the smoking wreckage.

More than an hour later, a filthy, ash-coated hand shot out of the rubble that had once been a house, the fingers moving back and forth like antennae scoping the surrounding area before venturing further.

Then another hand punched its way through, and within seconds, Mike's head appeared, covered with soot and dirt. In short order he was able to drag his body onto the top of the debris.

He lay there breathing heavily, staring up as the roaring fire behind him filled the sky with smoke. Numerous small fires burned here and there, as if some Cub Scouts had gone crazy with campfires.

Mike rolled onto his side and vomited, wracked by dry heaves. He hadn't eaten in days. In time his stomach settled and he sat up, dirt falling from his hair. He was amazed at the devastation. If he hadn't seen the plane coming down for himself, he would have thought Illinois had been bombed, perhaps by a rival country.

Coughing from all the dust and smoke, he stood up on unsteady legs. The wind was blowing the fire in all directions and if he stayed where he was, the conflagration would envelop him.

Climbing down off the pile of shattered wood beams and collapsed walls, he started shuffling, still too dazed to even think of where he was going. He looked up at the smoking Chicago skyline and it seemed to call to him.

Deciding the city was as good a place as any, he headed off in that direction, not sure what he'd find there but hoping it might be better than what he was leaving behind.

CHAPTER 7

Bill and the others walked quietly down the highway, each of them lost in private thoughts. Though wary of running into other people, so far they had seen no other survivors of the explosion.

The fires burned brightly behind them, turning the day into night as the ash from the flames floated higher into the sky. Hot embers floated on the breeze, landing on homes and structures that had escaped the brunt of the blast. Now these structures, too, caught fire, joining the massive conflagration as it slowly consumed everything east of Chicago.

Bill slowed his pace and walked backwards, letting the others move by him. Marie walked next to him, not wanting to be the first to break the silence. Bill did it for her.

"My house is in that hell back there somewhere," he said quietly.

"I'm sorry, Bill." That was all she could think to say.

He looked at her as if for the first time, and Marie realized he'd just been thinking aloud.

"Huh, what? Oh, thanks Marie. I know I shouldn't give a damn about my house, but it's one of the few things I have left that was both me and my wife's." He turned forward again and looked up at the sky. "Guess it all seems silly now."

Marie patted his arm. "That's not true and you know it. Without our history, we wouldn't know where we're going to in the future. One balances the other out."

Bill shrugged. "I suppose so. On the other hand, I guess there is a small bright side to all of this."

"Oh, and what could that possibly be?"

"Well, I did have a shitty mortgage. Interest was too damn high." His face lightened slightly. "Hey, I wonder if I'm covered under fire and falling airplanes."

Marie pursed her lips. "That's not funny, Bill, but I get your point."

"Yeah, I guess. Okay, but there is a real bright side to all of this."

"Okay, what is it?" she asked warily, wondering if he would crack another joke.

"Well, it's a chance to start over, I suppose, start new and fresh. That is, if we can make it to somewhere safe."

Marie stepped over a dented hubcap. "That's true, have you given it any thought? I mean, about where we'll go?"

"A little." He pointed to one of the numerous highway markers. "Right now we're on Highway 23. If we keep walking, we'll come to the junction for Route 113. There's a big industrial complex there. Everything from toilet paper to textiles. I figure when everything started to happen and people started getting sick and going crazy, they would have abandoned their jobs and gone home. Hopefully, the place is deserted."

Marie grinned. "Sure, sounds good to me. Should we check with the others, see if they're all on-board, or if anyone knows of a better place?"

Bill agreed and they caught up to some of the others. The first two people Bill passed were Bruce and Elizabeth. He had noticed them talking ever since everyone had abandoned the van. It looked like the two of them were hitting it off.

Bill approved.

If there was one thing the world needed right now, it was love. Since the viral outbreak, it seemed to be in short supply.

Bill and Marie checked with the others one at a time until everyone agreed upon the industrial complex, and they picked up the pace. A few cars lined the shoulder, some slanted at odd angles. The doors were closed, the engines silent. The small group moved past them with barely a glance.

From the front seat of an abandoned car, Kenny Atkinson watched the group of people walk by. He waited until the last person was far enough away he wouldn't be noticed, then reached into the back seat and shook Tessa Bateman's shoulder.

"What do you want?" Tessa mumbled. "It can't be my turn to stand watch."

"No, it's not that," Kenny said in a squeaky voice. He was on the verge of puberty and his voice seemed to change every hour. "A bunch of people just walked by and they didn't look like they were crazy. I heard them talking and stuff and they sounded fine."

Tessa sat up slowly, making sure the area around them was clear. Scratching her hair and yawning, she looked over the dashboard. Sure enough she could see a line of people moving down the highway. .

"Damn it, Kenny," she said, sitting up all the way, "why didn't you wake me when you first saw them? If they're okay like us, then we could have joined them."

Kenny leaned against the dashboard. "Well, shit, Tess, I didn't know what to do. What if they'd been crazies? I figured I'd let them pass and then wake you; that way there was no way they'd see me."

Tessa climbed out and looked behind the car. The fire was still burning brightly, the sun lost in ash-grey clouds. Luckily, she and Kenny had been on the road when the first explosion had rocked the earth. At first she'd thought it was an earthquake or a bomb. She still had no idea what had started the massive fire, but it really didn't matter. She knew there was no going back, that's for sure. She also knew there'd be no fire department to put out the inferno.

Tessa stretched her lithe frame and looked to the other end of the highway, where the people had just disappeared. The road had a slight incline to it, so the people seemed to evaporate from her vision, but she knew they weren't that far ahead.

She leaned forward in the seat, looking at her reflection in the car's rearview mirror. Her light brown hair was a mess, and her normally immaculate skin was streaked with dirt. But despite all these imperfections, any man would call her beautiful.

She had met Kenny completely by accident. After her parents went completely nutso, she'd managed to barricade her bedroom door and sneak out her window. After that she had continued running, realizing the streets weren't much safer than her home.

That night she hid in an abandoned bakery and stuffed herself on stale bread and pastries. That was where she found Kenny. His parents owned the shop, and when they had succumbed to the infection too, Kenny had run from their home only a few streets away to hide in the shop.

At first Kenny had been frightened of Tessa, had thought she was going to kill him, but after a lot of talking and reassurances that she was sane, he finally gave in.

Kenny had to be twelve or thirteen years old, only a few years younger than Tessa. The two had become friends quickly, both just glad to have someone to talk to.

They stayed in the bakery for the next day and a half, only sneaking out the back door when a crowd of crazies came into the bakery looking for food.

Tessa had studied this. Although they were all raving killers, apparently they still needed to eat. If they weren't intelligent enough to grow or raise food on their own, would it be just a matter of time before they died out?

Questions like these were what Tessa lived for. She'd always been a smart girl, had always asked questions. She was a straight-A student and had been planning on going to the college of her choice in another two years, though she figured that probably wouldn't be happening now.

"Are we going to follow them?" Kenny asked. He'd been talking before that, but she had ignored him. "Do you think they're going to the Army camp? Or maybe to the lab that guy told us about? The one in Centennial Park or whatever?"

Tessa reached into the front seat of the car and retrieved a small backpack. It contained all the food they had at the moment, and was more important to her than her Visa or cell phone. She thought it was funny how priorities could change on a dime.

She ruffled his hair. "Calm down, squirt. Yeah, we'll follow them. Hopefully they are what you said they are and they won't end up tearing us to pieces when we catch up to them; but if they're going to the camp then forget it."

According to rumors, a military camp had set up outside of Chicago. A few other survivors had told her the policy was to shoot on sight and ask questions later. Some of the survivors were nothing more than slaves, and others were test subjects for experiments. From the looks on the informants' faces, Tessa had no reason not to believe them. She had decided to stay as far from there as humanly possible.

Kenny folded his arms across his chest and scrunched up his face. "I know what I saw Tess, and they looked okay."

She opened the rear door and stepped onto the dusty shoulder of the highway, the odor of burnt rubber, wood and plastic filling the air.

Backing away from the car, she moved towards the hot pavement, always ready to jump back into the tall grass lining the highway if she spotted something dangerous.

"Well, I guess we'll find out either way then, huh?" She showed Kenny her back and began to walk away up the road like she was having a stroll in the park.

Kenny climbed out of the car and watched her. He puckered even more, as if he'd eaten the biggest, sourest lemon in the world. Then he kicked a rock and started to follow her.

"Girls," he said, and he jogged to catch up.

Mike had been walking for more than an hour when he looked over his shoulder. The highway had looped around and was now parallel with another road that meandered south, half a mile to his left.

He knew the area pretty well and remembered that the other road would curve away in another mile or so. There was a big industrial park out there somewhere. Nothing that could help him.

The highway he was on curved and sloped upward until he was a little higher than the other road, granting him an open view in all four directions. He looked around, made sure he wasn't being followed—and saw movement on the other road. Were those people?

Crouching, he ran along behind the guardrail. The position hurt his back, the bruises from when the house fell on him, but he ignored the pain. He watched the other group closely, too far away to make out faces.

He was about to give up and go his own way when a man in the back of the convoy walked over to the guardrail and gazed over the plain that separated the highways.

Mike stayed low. With the distance and the cover of the guardrail, he was vaguely sure he wouldn't be spotted. But he could see the other man just fine. And when the sun peeked out from a bank of ash-covered clouds, it illuminated the man's face.

Mike's jaw dropped. It was Bill. And a second later a woman walked up to him, and Mike could tell by the gray hair that it was that bitch, Marie.

So they hadn't died in the fireball like he'd thought.

Bill seemed to look around the plain, almost as if he could sense Mike out there, but then Marie tugged his arm and the couple continued on. But before Bill left the guardrail, Mike saw the flash of metal, the dim sunlight reflecting on the polished barrel of the .38.

Mike watched Bill move away down the road, then pushed himself up and jogged to the far right shoulder of the highway where no one could see him from the other road.

Finding them made no difference, he realized, and he continued on his own path down the highway.

The road began to curve to the right, toward Chicago. Mike spit into the gravel on the shoulder, cursing his luck for ever falling into Bill's bunch of assholes. Rubbing his crotch, he wished Becky was with him. After all he'd been through, he could use a good blowjob to let off some stress, and, man, could she do that like a pro.

Oh well, he thought, there would be plenty of pussy in Chicago. Hell, maybe he'd even see about doing one of the loonies. They might be crazy, but their bodies were still warm and soft.

He smiled, feeling like he had a purpose, a destination.

Yes sir, maybe splitting off from Bill and the others would turn out to be a good thing after all.

CHAPTER 10

"Shouldn't be too much farther now," Bill said when they passed a road sign for Centennial Park. "Sign says only two miles."

"Thank God, my feet are killing me," Melissa gasped.

A few other muffled groans filtered back to Bill as the rest of the group gave their two cents. They'd been walking for hours, what would have been a twenty-minute car ride.

Most of them were walking in a daze, simply concentrating on placing one foot in front of the other. Luckily, the sky had become overcast, threatening rain. Though a downpour wasn't exactly welcome, it was nice to have some cloud shelter from the sun. With the arrival of the first rain cloud, the temperature had dropped more than five degrees.

Bill could only hope they made it to the office park before the first raindrops fell.

Turning to check their back trail, Bill glimpsed a small fig-ure before it disappeared again. He grinned.

He didn't know who was following them, but he knew there were only two of them. And whoever they were, they certainly didn't act infected.

Marie noticed him grinning and moved closer. "Did you see them?" she asked.

He nodded slightly. "Yeah, they're still there. Think we should stop and introduce ourselves?"

Marie shook her head. "Nah, let them come when they're good and ready. They're just scared. Once they know we're friendly, I'm sure they'll come closer."

Bill was about to add something to that when a scream and a yell floated across the highway from behind him. Everyone turned, and Bill cursed under his breath.

Refugees from the fires had finally caught up to them. As they all watched from more than half a mile away, it was easy to see—even from this distance—the mass of people running down the middle of the highway were definitely infected. They didn't sneak around like the other people following Bill's group. Instead they jumped up and down and waved their arms wildly while crashing into each other. Some were badly burned, their clothes nothing but cinders, their single-mindedness to reach the survivors almost frightening in its intensity. Their howls preceded them.

Bill spotted the two people who'd been trailing them, now running from the horde of murderers nipping at their heels.

"Shit, we need to run for it, now!" he yelled, turning and dashing down the highway. "Make for the office park!"

The others followed him.

Bruce scooped Phillip up in his arms, carrying the five-year-old so he wouldn't be left behind.

The first mile passed under their feet in a blur of terror. Bill quickly realized every second they ran, every yard they tried to gain was for nothing; the horde would still catch them. Looking over his shoulder, he could clearly see the deranged faces as the crazies galloped and jumped, and it froze the blood in his veins.

Marie was one of the first to falter, her age and lack of real exercise slowing her down. Bill placed his arm around her, urging her on.

"No," she gasped, limping as fast as she could. "Go on without me, I'll only slow you down."

Unwilling to waste his breath arguing with her, he simply dragged her forward and said, "Shut up and run."

With less than half a mile to the office park, the two people who'd been trailing them caught up to the rest of the survivors.

Bill noticed they were nothing more than children, though on closer inspection the girl seemed to be closer to adulthood. No one welcomed them, but simply concentrated on running.

Elizabeth picked up a cramp, and if it wasn't for Bruce by her side, the woman would have. He wrapped his arm around her and almost carried her to keep her moving, Phillip still cradled in his other arm. Janice helped him, took one side so that they were almost carrying Elizabeth between them as they ran.

Tessa was in front of the group and was the first to spot the building at the beginning of Centennial Park.

She turned and called out to Bill. She didn't know him, but he acted like the leader. "Hey, we need to go over there! There might be help in one of those buildings!"

"What the hell are you talking about?" Bill asked. "Who are you?"

Tessa shook her head. "It doesn't matter right now. Just trust me, we need to go over to those buildings!"

"No kidding!" Bill snapped back.

He waved everyone over the guardrail and had them cut across the field separating the highway from the office complex.

With all of them on their last legs and the first of the raving killers almost on top of them, they ran full tilt into the complex. Bill surveyed the buildings, knowing he had only one chance to find an unlocked door. If he chose wrong, they would all be trapped as the horde surrounded them.

He quickly read the name on the side of each building: FOREST TEXTILES, MCCULLANE PHARMACEUTICALS ...

Someone behind him shrieked as the first of the infected prepared to grab Elizabeth and Bruce.

Pulling the .38 from his pants and releasing Marie to let her run ahead, Bill slowed his gait, and with an almost casual aim he sent a round at a raving man.

The bullet only grazed his shoulder, but it was enough to make him stumble.

Bruce and Elizabeth poured on their reserve strength and pulled away from the front of the mob. Bill turned and started running again.

His eyes caught the writing on a green awning over a doorway one hundred feet to his left. The words STAR LABS were stenciled in neat, white lettering on the awning, and he almost yelled in relief when he saw the door was partially open.

Tessa ran up next to him, pointing to the sign. "This is it; this is the one I heard about. We need to go in there. There should be help inside!"

Bill looked at the girl and weighed his options. The wrong choice wouldn't just get *him* killed. But he really had no choice.

"Over there!" he called to the others. "Go over there!" He grabbed Marie again and ran as fast as his waning strength would let him.

Pains shot up his left side and settled in his chest, and he wondered if he was about to have a heart attack.

Phillip's older brother Roger was the first to reach the doorway. He charged inside, and the others followed him one at a time. Bill pushed Marie into the building and then covered the others, popping the last few rounds in his revolver into the psychos to give his friends the few precious seconds they needed to get safe.

The screaming mob was packed so tight he hit a person with each round, causing the front of the line to falter for just an instant. One of the crazies fell to the grass in a tangle of arms and legs, and some directly behind him tripped. But it only halted them for a moment; the others simply climbed over the bodies as they tried to be the first to reach Bill and his group.

The young boy and girl were the last into the building, and Bill came right behind them.

No sooner than he had slammed the door, dozens of bodies banged against it. He slid the deadbolt in place and engaged the lock on the handle. He could see the door bending in its frame—it would only be a matter of time before it collapsed.

Blood began to seep under the bottom of the door as the mob crushed the first of the infected against the metal.

Bill stepped back from the slowly spreading pool of red and tried to swallow the knot in his throat. If he'd been slower or had tripped in his mad dash to safety, that could have been him out there, smashed into the building.

Keeping his eyes on the shaking door, he kept walking backward, only stopping when his heel struck someone lying on the floor. He glanced down to see Marie, her shirtless chest heaving, her slim frame drenched in sweat. All of them had managed to run almost two miles nonstop, fueled only by terror and adrenaline. Everyone had collapsed to the floor.

Bill dropped down next to Marie. She flashed him a wan smile, her breath coming in gasps. "Thank you," she said, and she caressed his cheek.

Bill took her hand and squeezed gently. "My pleasure." The he closed his eyes and concentrated on breathing. The pains in his chest were subsiding and he realized he would probably be okay.

"You know," he said between gasps of air, "I'm getting far too old for this shit."

Marie giggled and nodded. The laughter was contagious and soon the others joined in. Phillip and Roger didn't even know what was so funny, but they laughed all the same, just glad to be alive.

For the moment, the banging on the door and the rest of the crazy world was irrelevant. Only sucking in the next lungful of air seemed to matter. At the edge of the group, both Kenny and Tessa moved closer together. They had no idea who these survivors were, but at the moment, with escape impossible, it appeared they were stuck with them.

CHAPTER 11

Dean leaned back in his self-made throne and grinned to himself. He'd cleared out the entire first floor of a clothing outlet, the room now one giant foyer leading to his throne at the back of the store.

To his right stood seven hostages, each one bound and gagged and tied to one of a dozen metal poles that supported the roof. All seven captives had tears in their eyes, though some were still too shocked to fully comprehend their situation.

Scattered across the white tile at their feet were the body parts and entrails of hostage number eight. The old man had been a screamer and Dean had enjoyed torturing him in front of the others. He'd cherished the fear in their eyes almost as much as he'd enjoyed ripping the old man apart limb by limb.

The old man's eyelids were still open, his decapitated head staring at the ceiling as if asking God why this had happened to him.

Dean leaned back in his oversized chair and smiled.

He remembered a saying from before, when he was a normal. "It's good to be the king," he said. In fact, it was downright awesome.

Leaning forward on his throne, he pointed to the hostage on the right, second from the end. She was a pretty little thing in her early thirties. Her blue eyes were wide with terror, and he relished every second of it.

The Changed surrounding him saw where he pointed and immediately did his bidding. They untied her and threw her to the floor at his feet.

"Please, why are you doing this to us?" the woman asked between sobs.

Dean stood up and walked the three stairs down from his throne. The woman was still lying on the ground, too frightened to move. Dean stepped on her neck. With just a slight amount of pressure, he could snap her spine, as easy as blowing out a candle. But what would be the fun in that? No, he wanted to make her suffer.

Releasing her neck, he knelt down so his lips were almost touching her ear.

"You want to know why I'm doing this? Well, I'll tell you. Before I was changed, I was nobody. People barely acknowledged my existence. But now I'm a king. These people listen to me, obey me without question. So why do I do what I do? Because I can, my dear, because I can."

He stood and ordered two of the Changed to rip off her clothes. She cried and fought, but only halfheartedly. She knew she was doomed.

Dean stripped.

Just before he mounted her, he called one of his more intelligent underlings, a disheveled woman who attentively awaited his instructions.

"Go out and find more normals. This can't be it. Take half of the men and women in here with you. Now go!"

The woman grunted and disappeared into the crowd, slapping men and women on the shoulder as she went, recruiting others to do Dean's bidding.

As the hall cleared out, Dean penetrated the woman, wrapped his hands around her neck and squeezed.

Her eyes bulged as she tried to breathe, the fear so strong Dean could smell it like a perfume. It mixed with the smell of tears as the other hostages either cried for the woman or wept for themselves, and Dean realized something. He held their very lives in his hands, could strike terror in them with a simple word. So perhaps he wasn't a king ... perhaps he was a god.

He felt himself climaxing. Without realizing it, he squeezed too hard and crushed the woman's throat. He only noticed when she stopped wriggling beneath him.

Dean backed away from the corpse. He kicked her, but she didn't stir.

"Damn it." Dean pointed to one of the Changed, a haggard looking man in his forties. "You, take her away. Feel free to have some fun with her; she's still warm."

The man nodded and grinned like an idiot. He dragged her away by the ankle, a few others following him.

Dean dressed and returned to his throne, where he looked down on the six other hostages, each one watching his every move.

"Now look, I know what you folks are thinking and it's really not that bad. After all, she's already dead." He grinned malevolently. "Just think of it as recycling for the new world." He started laughing, and his underlings echoed him. Pretty soon the store was filled with cackles and chuckles as the Changed laughed and hooted with their king.

Mike slowed as he approached the city limits of Chicago. Across the highway was a military convoy, the trucks parked so that nothing could enter or exit the city without going by the barricade.

Raising the large lead pipe he'd found on the side of the road, he moved a little closer. Nothing moved; the bodies scattered around the barrier appeared to be dead.

All the soldiers wore white biohazard suits, though their gas masks were spread around them on the pavement like discarded beer cans at a frat party. All the bodies had been ripped apart, the wounds looking like a pack of hyenas or wild dogs had attacked them.

When he was no more than a few feet away from the first body, his eyes caught the reflection of the soldier's M-16 still lying under the corpse. With his heart fluttering in his throat, he moved the last few feet warily and snatched up the weapon. The body rolled onto its side and Mike jumped two feet in the air, thinking the soldier was about to attack him. But when the body remained still, he knew the man was dead.

Though not an expert with firearms Mike had enough rudimentary knowledge to figure out how to eject the clip and find the safety.

The magazine was empty. Whatever had happened here, at least the soldier had given as good as he'd gotten. Mike searched the soldier's body, finding another full magazine. He slapped it into the empty weapon and racked the arming bolt, sending the first round into the chamber. Feeling better now that he was armed, he climbed over the bumpers of two trucks parked nose to nose to block traffic.

When he was on top of the trucks, he paused for a moment, taking in the visceral sight on the other side. If he had wondered where the soldier had expended his rounds, he now had his answer.

Bodies littered the street surrounding the barricade, all lying in odd directions where they had fallen. Infected and white-suited soldiers alike covered the ground, so it would be difficult to traverse the street without tripping over a corpse. Flies and insects were everywhere, buzzing happily in the spilt blood. A murder of crows hopped from body to body, searching for tender eyes and soft tissue to feed on. One particular crow poked its head up and glared at Mike when he stepped on the bumpers of the trucks, its single eye hanging by a few threads.

Mike started counting corpses and stopped when he'd reached more than one hundred. Evidently, the military had tried to contain the infected in the city and had failed miserably.

Looking at all the bodies spread out before him, and the empty city spread out in front of him, he realized maybe coming into Chicago was a bad idea.

He jumped back down onto the road, already deciding he'd go somewhere else when he spotted movement out of the corner of his eye. Before he realized what was happening, dozens of infected people came from around the trucks and from the nearby streets. Mike raised the rifle, squeezing the trigger again and again, forgetting the safety was on. He started shaking the rifle, confused.

The nearest infected lunged at him, and he swung the rifle butt-first, shattering the man's jaw, knocking him to the street unconscious. That was when Mike found the safety on the M-16 and flicked it off with his thumb.

The rifle vibrated in his hand, spitting death, his shoulder absorbing some of the kick as the weapon's muzzle inched toward the sky. Mike overcompensated for the climb, aimed too low, the bullets tearing into the asphalt in front of the infected horde.

A few of the attacking crowd were shot in the feet and legs, but in seconds they knocked Mike over, sent the rifle flying from his hands to clatter in the street.

He screamed, tried to fight them off. He expected to feel teeth and hands ripping into his flesh, but a sharp voice barked for the attackers to stop.

"No, no kill," the man said from the middle of the crowd. "Bring to king!"

"Holy shit, you guys can talk?" Mike asked despite his terror. He was surrounded on all sides, and if he'd even entertained the idea of escape, he would have easily been brought down and killed.

The man didn't respond, just grunted and pointed back into the city. The infected pushed Mike back over the trucks and onto the city side of the highway.

He came down hard on something squishy. At first he didn't want to look, but as he sat up, he found he'd landed inside the body cavity of a slain soldier. His right arm was wrist-deep in viscera, the organs and tissue twining around his already shaking limb. With a yell of disgust and terror, he rolled away from the corpse, shaking the blood and bile from his hand as he went. Before he knew it he was pulled to his feet, and the mob of raving and screaming people pushed him deeper into Chicago.

While he walked, Mike looked at the stores and buildings around him. A McDonald's was missing all its windows, the Burger King next to it in a similar state. A record store and a UPS store were still smoking from an old fire. The smell of smoke and burning debris was everywhere, and on the other end of the city flames reached high into the sky. Mike wondered how long it would take with the right amount of wind before the blaze spread throughout the city.

They'd walked so far he was totally lost. He never went into the city very often, so its layout was a mystery to him. Bodies littered the streets and sidewalks, their eyes staring at nothing. Walking close to the corpse of a woman, Mike noticed the skin on her face was rippling. He almost vomited when a score of cockroaches spewed out of her mouth and nose.

Rats scurried everywhere, enjoying all the free meat just lying out in the open. A few small rodents were eating the eyes of a corpse lying on the hood of a car. When the crowd was only a few feet away, the rats reared up on their hind legs and screeched at the intruders. Then each one ran away with a succulent eyeball or other choice bit and disappeared under a nearby postal truck, its doors opened, mail blowing everywhere.

A letter skated across the road and landed at Mike's feet. He read the black script on the cover and almost wanted to laugh. It said he could be a millionaire if he just opened the letter. The top edge of the letter was a deep scarlet, and a small gobbet of flesh stuck to the corner. A few insane titters escaped his lips, but he managed to control himself, his stomach spasming from fear and dread. Only sheer force of will kept him from vomiting all over his sneakers.

Fifteen minutes later, the crowd halted in front of a clothing store. Mike noticed all the windows were intact, one of the few ground floor structures to retain its glass. He was pushed toward the main entrance and was shoved through the swinging door. He tripped over his feet and fell heavily onto the polished marble.

Multiple hands dragged him deeper into the store. Though he wanted to fight, he knew it was hopeless. Whatever they were going to do with him, he could only hope it was quick.

With his feet dragging behind, he was pulled through racks of clothing until he reached an open space. The racks had all been removed, creating something like a grand ballroom.

He was picked up and placed on his feet again, and a hand pushed him to the foot of what looked like a throne. The large, high-backed chair was made out of boxes and crates held together with duct tape. Mike tried not to look at the remains of six bodies lying to his right.

The man sitting in the throne stood up and walked down the stairs.

"Well done, my people, you have done well bringing me another plaything." He pointed to the closest metal post. "Tie him over there."

Mike was grabbed from all angles and pushed and dragged to the metal post. His arms were pulled behind him hard, causing him to yelp in pain.

The man walked over to him, chuckling. "Already in pain? My friend, you don't know what pain is, but I promise you will find out."

"Who the hell are you?" Mike asked. "You aren't like them, why don't you help me?"

"Oh, but I am like them. Except for some reason I can still think, I'm still me—only better. I'm one of the new breed, the Changed. The military tried to quarantine us, tried to keep us in, but I think you know what happened to them."

Mike stared into the man's deranged eyes. If he wasn't crazy, then Mike didn't know what crazy was.

"Now, even as we speak, I'm burning the city to the ground, and any normals still alive will run to me like rats. When I'm done, every normal in the Chicago area will be dead, and then I'll spread out until the whole damn country is mine. But don't you worry; you won't be around to see it." He raised his right hand and scratched Mike's face.

His ragged fingernails cut deep into Mike's cheek, causing him to cry out. The mob laughed and roared, enjoying his suffering. Blood dripped onto his bare chest. As the blood rolled down into his pants, he started to shiver, about to let go of his bladder.

The crazy man raised his hand again, preparing to strike Mike.

"Wait!" Mike cried. "Don't kill me! I know where there's other people like me!"

The man arched his eyebrows. "I'm listening."

Mike looked over at the corpses piled carelessly in the corner and swallowed deeply. "You've got to promise you won't kill me. I'll help you, I swear, and I'll do whatever you say. I know where there's almost a dozen people!"

The man rubbed his jaw, thinking it over. "You know, I have to admit it would be nice to have someone to talk to, someone that actually knew what the hell I was saying. A lapdog, a right-hand man. You know what, sure okay, why not?" He leaned closer to Mike as if he was a confidant. "Besides, if I get bored with you, I can always kill you."

Mike nodded his head. "Sure, okay, that's fine, but I promise you won't be sorry."

The man stepped back and gestured to Mike, ordering one of the Changed to untie him. Free, Mike stepped away from the pole, rubbing his wrists. He reached up and touched his cheek, the deep scratch already clotting.

The man held out his hand to Mike. "My name's Dean, Dean Carlson, and I'm the new king of Chicago."

Mike hesitantly took his hand. "Mike Fogarty."

Dean placed an arm around Mike's shoulders and started walking to the front door. "So, Mike Fogarty, start talking, and if I don't like what I hear then you'll be back on that post before you finish your last word."

CHAPTER 12

Bill rolled to his feet, deciding he'd spent enough time recovering. They were far from in the clear, the door still shaking like hellhounds were trying to gain entry.

"All right, everyone, that's enough rest for now. You can rest more when you're dead. Right now we need someone to find something to put against that door. And the sooner the better."

Bruce rose to his feet, already moving out of the small hallway they had fallen into after entering the building. "I'm on it. Elizabeth, you want to help me?"

She nodded and the couple disappeared around a bend in the hallway.

Bill watched the door rattle in its frame; he was pretty sure it would hold—at least long enough for them to decide on a course of action.

"All right, people, on your feet. I know you're all tired, but we need to see what's in here and figure out how we're going to get out of this place in one piece."

Moans and groans filled the hallway as everyone rose on unsteady legs. Bill knew how they felt. Though he tried to stay relatively fit, going for walks after dinner and such, even *his* legs were sore after their two-mile dash down the highway.

Marie was using the wall to hold herself up, and she shot him a weak smile. "Don't worry about this old broad; she's still got some life in her yet."

A loud screeching sound filled the hallway behind him, and he turned to see Bruce and Elizabeth pushing a heavy metal desk across the floor, leaving long scratches in their wake. The two struggled to keep the desk moving over the grout lines in the tiles.

Melissa and Janice joined in, and in no time the desk was planted against the door.

Bill nodded. "That's good. But one more on top would be better.

"That's no problem, there's a room full of them back there."

"All right then, what are we waiting for?" Bill moved down the hall, following the scratches on the floor.

He stepped inside a large room used for office cubicles. Neck-high cork walls separated each one. Bill grabbed the next desk in line and started pushing it out into the hallway. Bruce was there a moment later, and the two men made quick work of lifting the desk onto the other against the door.

"It should do," Bill said, stepping away from their haphazard barricade. "At least until we're ready to go."

Bruce just grunted, then turned away to join the others.

At the end of the long hall was a small breakroom, which also served as the cafeteria. Marie was already opening packages of noodles, and others were munching on candy bars. The survivors had shattered the glass front of a vending machine in the corner and were eagerly taking out its contents. The soda machine proved more difficult to open, and Bill thought it the biggest irony that he actually had to put money in the machine to buy a Coke.

He handed the can to Phillip, and the young boy smiled. Bill thought that was the sweetest thing. Have a Coke and a smile, just like the commercials said.

Though things were bad, he couldn't imagine what it must all look like to a child, watching the adults battle for their lives in a world turned upside down.

"We need to set a watch; someone needs to keep an eye on that door. If it starts to give, we need to know before they get in here." He looked around the room. "So who's first?"

All the survivors were silent, each concentrating on eating. Finally, when it seemed no one would volunteer, Melissa raised her hand. "Oh, fine, I'll go first. Christ, what is this, kindergarten?"

"I'm in kindergarten," Phillip said from the corner of the room, where he was eating a candy bar with the Coke Bill had given him. "My teacher's name is Mrs. Milton."

At first no one knew what to say, everyone so surprised to hear the boy talk. He'd said nothing since arriving at the school days ago, along with his brother.

Marie walked over to him and gently rubbed his hair. "Of course it is, dear. And I'm sure she's a great teacher."

"Will I ever get to see her again?" Phillip asked.

"Um, I don't know, honey. I sure hope so."

Melissa stood up, her chair scraping across the tile. Wiping her hands on her pants, she moved to the door leading from the breakroom.

"Thanks, Melissa," Bill said. "I'll have someone relieve you in an hour or so."

She answered with a quick wave and was gone, her footsteps echoing down the hall. Janice handed Bill a granola bar, and he took it with a smile. Chewing, he sat down.

"Look, guys," he said, "we're not safe in here. Once we rest up, we need to figure out how to ditch those bastards and go somewhere better. More secure."

"And where is that, exactly?" Janice asked from across the table. "Those damn nuts are everywhere, Bill. Where the hell are we supposed to go? How can we fight a whole city?"

"I heard something about the military setting up a temporary camp outside of Chicago on the TV before I left my house," Elizabeth said. "Maybe we could find out where they are and go there."

"I know where they are," a small voice said from the back of the room. It was the first time Bill had heard her voice, and he realized no one had been introduced to their new arrivals.

"And who might you be? With all the commotion we never got properly introduced. I'm Bill and that's Marie, for starters."

"Well first off," she said, "I'm Tessa and this is Kenny."

Everyone said hi, and a round of introductions was made. Bill walked over to Tessa and sat down next to her.

"Okay, so now that we all know one another, what were you saying about there being help in this place? And do you know where the refugee camp is?"

"Uh-huh, sort of, but I don't want to go there. They scared us, me and Kenny. The soldiers wear these scary white jumpsuits and have gas masks on. But the worst thing is they shoot everyone on sight. If you went too close to their camp, they just shot you, whether you were one of the crazy people or not. At least that's what we heard."

"Sounds like they're scared," Bruce said around a mouthful of Twinkie.

"And who isn't?" Janice asked. "If this infection or plague or whatever keeps spreading, then the whole world could possibly collapse. But I don't see anywhere else we can go."

Bill nodded and turned to Tessa.

"Okay, fine, so we know about the camp. Now what about this building? What's so special about it?

Tessa shrugged. "I don't know really, but I heard a story from one of the people there. He said he was a scientist. Well, actually he said he worked in a place called Star Labs. He said they were working with viruses and stuff. I just took a chance that this was the right place."

Bill's eyebrows went up in surprise. "You took a chance?"

Tessa nodded, looking timid with so many eyes on her.

Janice sat taller and tapped her right hand on the table to get the other's attention. "We need to go to the camp. Where else is there to go?"

Bill nodded. "She's right. Despite the fact we might be turned away—or worse, shot—we need to try. It's either that or just stay here until either we run out of food or those bastards break in."

Everyone started arguing and talking at once. Finally, Bill slammed his hands on the table and stood up. "All right, okay, wait a minute. Now we don't have to decide right now. But we do need to make a decision quickly. So let's all sleep on it, okay? We all need rest, real rest, and now's the time with a roof over our heads. Once we've rested a little more, we can see if what Tessa said about this place is correct."

Everyone agreed, and some left the breakroom for the hallway while others stayed.

After a half hour, everyone looked better, their complexions more normal thanks to a small sense of being safe inside the walls of the building. Bill spoke up again, gathering everyone back into the breakroom.

"All right then, now that we've all rested, what do you say we explore, see what's in here. Especially with what Tessa said earlier. Though I've got to tell you, Tessa, this place looks deserted."

When everyone was finished eating, they paired up in groups of two. Bill grinned when he saw Bruce and Elizabeth pairing up.

As they were all moving down the hall to explore, Bill called to them one last time. "Try to find some weapons! Anything we can use!"

Turning back into the breakroom, Bill saw Marie leaning against the wall while both Phillip and his brother Roger sat at the table below her. "I figured I'd keep these two guys with me," she said.

Bill shrugged. "Sure, whatever." He looked over at Tessa and Kenny. "What about you two? You want to hang with us?"

Kenny seemed to like the idea.

"Sure, whatever," Tessa said, parroting Bill's answer to Marie. Her eyes drifted to Roger, about the same age as her; she looked away bashfully.

Bill chuckled. Even in such dire circumstances, the human heart still looked for companionship, whether it was Bruce and Elizabeth or Tessa eyeing Roger.

"Well, come on gang," Bill said, heading into the hall "let's see what Star Labs has to show us."

CHAPTER 13

Bill and Marie, along with the three children, walked down the deserted, debris-strewn hallway; Roger had decided to stay in the breakroom and Bill had agreed it was all right.

Doors lined each side of the hall, some open, others closed. Bill slowed when he came upon a door marked, "Bio-genetics, Authorized Personnel Only." Below that sign was another with smaller lettering that read, "Keep badges in view at all times."

"This one looks interesting," he said. The door was already ajar, so he pushed it all the way open and stepped inside. The second he stepped over the threshold, the stink of death struck him in the face. He held his arms out to his sides to stop the others from coming into the room.

"Marie, why don't you wait here with the kids until I make sure it's safe?"

"Be careful," she said, pulling Phillip closer to her. The boy didn't resist.

Bill stepped into the room. There was a desk nearby, and on the desk in a holder for pens and pencils was a letter opener, a better weapon than his empty .38. He picked it up and moved deeper into the office.

Similar to the room Bruce had found, the large open space was divided into cubicles. Bill moved down the main aisle, expecting something or someone to jump out at him any second.

Reaching the end of the space, he saw a leg lying on the floor, the rest of the body hidden from view. With the letter opener in front of him, he moved closer and looked inside. He immediately turned away, covering his nose with his bare arm.

He knew he had to take a closer look. For weapons or anything useful. They all needed new clothes since they made that rope to escape the mall, but Bill didn't want to wear anything off a corpse. Besides, the body's clothes were bloody and ripped. Bill assumed it had once been a man, thanks to the shoes, but he couldn't tell because the head was a shattered mess of bone and brain matter squirming with maggots. Both arms had been pulled from the body, like the man had been drawn and quartered, but the legs were left intact.

On the man's bloodstained white coat was an ID badge. Holding his breath, Bill leaned over and plucked the badge from the man's pocket, shaking maggots off the card. He quickly moved away from the corpse, almost running back to Marie and the others.

Now halfway across the room, with the odor of rotting meat behind him, he noticed the air smelled almost sweet.

"Found this," he said, handing the badge to Marie as he stepped into the hallway. The sounds of pounding floated down the hall, the infected still doing their best to break inside the building.

"What are we supposed to do with this?" Marie asked, but it was Tessa who took the badge from her and looked at it more closely.

"I've seen these before, or something like it at my school. They just started using them. See this black line?" She pointed to the magnetic strip on the bottom of the badge. "I'll bet anything it's to get you into somewhere."

"You think that's an access card?" Bill asked, taking the badge from her and looking at it again. Now that he was in the hall, away from the smell of death, he could think more clearly.

Tessa nodded. "It's got to be. The question is, where's the door it opens? Do you think it's the one the scientist was talking about?"

Bill stared at the card for a moment, thinking. "She's probably right," he said, enjoying the little mystery they'd discovered. "Okay then, let's split up, look for a card reader outside one of the hall doors. Odds are that'll be the one."

Elizabeth poked her head out of a door on the far side of the hallway and waved. "Hey, guys, guess what we found. A whole locker room full of clothes, probably from the employees that worked here before they took off. Guess they left in a hurry and didn't change."

"Hey, that's great," Bill called. "Listen, keep your eye out for a locked door with a card reader next to it, okay?"

"Sure, no problem. See ya." She popped back in the room, disappearing like a ghost.

Bill looked at the others and grinned. "Well, what are we waiting for? Let's see if we can find that room."

Fifteen minutes later, Marie called from two hallways over with Phillip by her side. Bill, Tessa and Roger, who had left the breakroom to join the search, jogged over. Phillip pointed at the closed door with the card reader next to it. Bill smiled; evidently, the boy was coming out of his shell. Bill could only hope to prevent more bad things from happening to him, or to any of them for that matter.

"Excellent, Marie, great job." Bill held up the badge. "Now to see if the slipper fits the right foot, said the Prince." He slid the card through the reader, and the red light quickly changed to green. The door hissed for a second and popped open.

Tessa stepped inside the room.

Bill grabbed for her, but she was out of his reach. "Damn it, Tessa, wait—it could be dangerous!"

"It's fine. I'm fine. Come on in. Wow, you've got to see this stuff."

"Well, what do you think?" Marie asked Bill.

"I think she's reckless and stupid, but I guess if there was going to be a problem it would have happened by now. So let's go see what she's found."

Bill stepped into the room with Marie and the kids right behind him. The first thing Bill noticed was how bright it was in the room. More than two dozen halogen lamps hung from the ceiling, washing away all the shadows.

The second thing he noticed was the cages filled with dead animals.

He was surprised there was almost no odor, until he saw the large vents on the walls and ceiling. With the air on full, the room was well ventilated. He didn't want to imagine what would happen if the power cut off.

The room was huge, about the size of a professional basketball court, only square. While he walked through the center aisle following Tessa between cages of dead animals, he wondered what they could have been doing in here. What kind of experiments would require such a broad spectrum of animals? He saw the typical lab animals, such as mice and rabbits, but there were multiple cages filled with dogs, cats and even a goat, all dead.

"What the hell were they doing in here?" Bill asked. "It looks like a damn pet store."

"Well, usually they test cosmetics and vaccines on test animals, but this? I have no idea," Marie said, holding Phillip tightly to her chest. "Maybe they were using the animals to test the virus. Makes sense. Human trials are always the last thing when testing for a cure."

Ahead of them, Tessa stopped at the far wall, marveling at the table full of beakers and test tubes. She leaned down and stared at the multicolored glass, her face distorting and magnifying in her reflection. "This place is so cool. It totally blows the lab at my school away."

"Aww, it ain't so great," Kenny said, speaking up for the first time.

Bill looked down at him. "Don't you like science, Kenny?"

He shrugged. "Guess so. But I'm not that good at it, so ... you know."

Bill nodded, remembering his days in school. "Yeah, I know what you mean."

Off against the far wall were half a dozen large hydrogen and oxygen tanks. The large cylinders always reminded Bill of torpedoes.

Looking closer at the dead animals, he guessed some of them died from starvation and dehydration. When everyone evacuated, there was no one left to take care of them. He shook his head, imagining the misery the poor creatures had suffered.

"Hey, I found something!" Tessa called from the corner of the room, hidden from view behind the cages.

The others caught up to her and stopped when she showed them what she'd discovered. In the corner of the room was another door, solid metal with a square window set high in the middle. This door, too, had a card reader and Bill swiped the card, nervous when the door released air with a hiss and slid open like something out of *Star Trek*.

"This looks important," he said. "Look at the rubber seals that line the frame. This is like one of those rooms in the *China Syndrome*. If they were testing vaccines and working with viruses, this has got to be where they did it."

"But here?" Marie asked. "In Illinois?"

"Sure," Tessa said, "the government loves to set up in unassuming places. That way no one suspects a thing. And that was why that scientist was in the camp. He must have come from here."

"My, aren't we a conspiracy nut. And so young," Bill said, grinning.

She shrugged. "It was mostly my dad, but I used to pay attention. Sometimes the stuff he found on the Internet made sense." She frowned slightly. "You know, Bill, not all conspiracies are false. There's a lot of them that are true; people just don't want to believe their government would do stuff like what was happening in this lab."

Marie leaned over and touched Bill's arm, eyeing the chamber warily. "Do you think we should go in there? I mean, what if we end up letting out some kind of virus, like the bubonic plague or SARS or anthrax?" Marie asked, hovering near the door. "I think we've got enough trouble already without adding more to the mix."

"Look, Marie, once the seal is broken it's already too late. If there was something in there that was going to hurt us, we'd already be dead, so I say what the hell. If you want, we can send the kids back to the breakroom."

"I'd like that," she said. "They don't need to see this, especially Phillip." She brushed her hand over the boy's hair.

"No way am I leaving," Kenny protested. "I want to see what's in there."

Bill sighed. "Jesus," he mumbled, "I hate kids." He looked to Kenny. "Hey, what do you say you bring Phillip back with you? It'll be a big favor to me. I'll make it up to you, I promise."

Kenny shrugged, disappointed. "Oh, okay. I could care less what's in that stupid room, anyway. Come on, Phillip, let's go get some more candy from the breakroom." He turned to look at Tessa. "You'll tell me what's in there later, though, right?"

Tessa shrugged like she was thinking about it.

"Forget it then, I changed my mind. I want to stay here."

"I want to see, too," Phillip said.

Bill pointed to the way out of the room. "No deal, Kenny. Now get going. I promise, if it's safe you can come back later. You too, Phillip."

Kenny hesitated, but Bill gave him a look that would brook no more argument. With a slumping of shoulders, the boy gave in. "This sucks. Even when everything's all crazy I still get left out of stuff." He and Phillip started walking away, and Bill followed them for a few feet to make sure they continued moving.

"Be careful, you two. And don't do anything but go straight back to the breakroom. We'll be there soon."

Kenny waved without looking back, and Marie chuckled. "My, what a way you have with children. Will you really let them come back if it's safe?"

Bill shrugged. "Doubt it, but at least Phillip seems to be getting better. At least he's talking now."

"Perhaps it's the arrival of Tessa and Kenny?"

"Maybe. Who knows what's going through his mind? Or Roger's for that matter."

"Hello," Tessa said impatiently. "Are we going in or what?"

"All right, hold your horses. Let the old folk talk a moment, will ya?"

Tessa answered by stomping her feet.

"Shall we?" Bill asked Marie, holding out his arm as if they were going dancing.

"Why, thank you, sir, I guess we shall." Marie took his arm and they both stepped through the pressurized door.

Tessa rolled her eyes and wondered why adults had to act so weird. Then she, too, went inside the chamber.

CHAPTER 14

Stepping inside the airlock, Bill saw another door in front of them.

"We need to close the outer door before the inner one will open," he told the others. "It's a safety feature."

Marie turned to her side and spotted a button on the wall. She pushed it, and the outer door closed with the hiss of hydraulics; once the chamber was re-pressurized, the inner door slid open, releasing the smell of disinfectant and stale death.

With the letter opener in front of him, Bill stepped into a smaller room, less than half the size of the one they'd vacated.

It reminded him of something out of a mad scientist's handbook. The tables were covered with more beakers and test tubes, and in the center of the room a computer terminal was affixed to the middle of a large desk. A chair lay on its side near the door, but otherwise the room appeared to be undisturbed.

Marie walked over to the desk and sat down. Bill moved with her and turned suddenly when Tessa shrieked. He held the letter opener ready to slash anything that moved. Tessa was fine;

she was looking at something on the floor of the room, hidden behind a large table.

Bill peeked around the desk and saw another dead animal, this one curled up in a ball. The dog's tan coat had shrunk tight around its ribs. Its eyelids were open, staring into the void. Bill leaned forward and turned its dog collar so he could read it better.

"SUBJECT 11524B," it read in bold, black type.

Bill placed his hand on Tessa's arm. "Looks like they might have made this one a pet," he said. "If I had to guess, I'd say the poor thing died from starvation. Come on, let's go back and join Marie, see what she's found."

Tessa nodded and let Bill lead her back to the center of the room. Marie looked up, curious about what had happened.

"It's nothing," Bill said. "Just another dead animal, maybe the lab's pet dog."

"Oh, okay. Well you won't believe what I've found. The computer was still logged in, so it was easy to surf the menus. Otherwise, I would never have been able to crack the password."

"Don't look at me. I have enough trouble just trying to read my e-mails," Bill said, looking over her shoulder at the flickering screen.

Tessa let out a huff. "Old people. Bill, get with the times."

Marie chuckled. "Yeah, Bill, either catch up or get out of the way. My daughter bought me a computer a few years ago and I taught myself how to use it. It's actually quite simple once you get the hang of it. Windows inside of other windows ... it's quite amazing actually. In fact—"

Bill cut her off. "Marie, please, a computer lesson later, okay? What did you find?"

"Well, I was able to access a video feed from a few days ago. Apparently it was a security camera that caught all the action, and it was supposed to be downloaded to the central processor, but that never happened. It's not long, but it's quite shocking. Are you ready?"

"Go, will ya? Hit the button, start the show."

Marie pressed a few keys and started the video. The picture was grainy, but it was easy to see everything that was happening.

A man in a biological containment suit, complete with oxygen tank on his back, moved across the floor of the lab. Without realizing it, the man accidentally knocked a beaker onto the floor, shattering the glass.

A moment later lights began to flash and the people in the room with him began to run. Just before the inner door slammed shut, a man pushed a chair in the frame, stopping the chamber from sealing. He quickly waved to the five others in the room, and one at a time they hopped over the chair, crowding into the airlock.

Then he kicked the chair away from the door and it slammed shut; the airlock cycled through and the men ran out of the airlock and disappeared off camera. Before the last one was gone, Bill could clearly see a large tear in the side of his white suit.

Marie hit a button and the picture went back to a screen saver. The picture of a gold star with the name *STAR LABS* inside bounced around the screen.

Bill looked away and dry-washed his face with his hands. "Jesus Christ, if what we saw is true, then those idiots let loose whatever was in that vile. This is where it all started."

"So what are you trying to say, Bill?" Marie asked.

"It's obvious, isn't it? Those damn scientists weren't trying to find a cure; they were the ones who made the virus in the first place. Goddamn idiots, they were messing with shit man has no right playing with."

Marie took his arm and squeezed gently, trying to comfort him. "It's all true, Bill, there's a time stamp on the video. It coincides with only a few days before things started getting bad out there. Whatever they let loose spread in only a few days."

"But what was it?" Tessa asked, leaning on the desk. "Some kind of plague?"

"I don't think so, honey. In fact, I found a video diary of one of the scientists, but I haven't looked at them yet. Should I call them up?"

Bill shrugged, still trying to wrap his head around what he'd seen. He was standing at ground zero. Pandora's Box, he was actually standing inside Pandora's Box.

"Shit, do you think we're in danger of getting infected in here?" he asked.

Marie shook her head. "Doubt it. Whatever was in here is out there in the air now—it's everywhere. Whatever this bug is, it seems we're immune." She turned back to the computer screen. "So do you want to see the video diary or what?"

"Sure, why the hell not. How bad could it be?"

Marie stroked the keys and another menu appeared along with a column of dates and names.

"Which one do you want to see?"

Bill read some of the names on the screens. "What about that one? *Dead-Rage*, it says; try that one. Doesn't matter really. Try something about a week ago, before all the shit hit the fan."

Marie highlighted the appropriate file. A second later a man's face filled the screen. He was short, maybe five foot five judging by his height relative to the tables around him. He had brown hair and brown eyes. The man removed his wire rim glasses for a moment, polishing them on his lab coat, and Bill could see the indentation on his nose where the eyewear sat.

The man flipped through a notebook and then spoke for the first time, his voice sounding hollow through the computer speakers.

"This is Dr. Theodore Donaldson, video log follow-up for the *Dead-Rage virus*. I've given the feline the injection and have been waiting five minutes for the first sign. I've placed the animal in the same cage as its mother. Before the initial injection, the cat was totally subservient to its parent, the mother being the dominant personality. But observe what occurred once the virus became active." The camera swung to a large glass cage where two orange and yellow cats sat inside, both docile.

"The mother is on the right, the infected feline on the left," the man said off-camera.

Bill, Marie and Tessa watched silently. At first the infected cat merely licked its mother, but after a few minutes it slowly grew more aggressive until finally it attacked with claws and teeth. The mother tried to defend herself, her claws out and her tail doubling in size, but she finally succumbed to death from too many bloody wounds. The infected cat never stopped attacking her, even after she was dead.

Finally, a hand reached over and turned a knob. Smoke filled the glass cage and the violent animal slowed its attack and dropped to the cage floor. Bill could see its chest rising and falling slowly; the animal had been gassed to sleep.

The camera swung back to the man's face and his eyes were wide with excitement. "It works, the virus works! This could mean so much. Once we adapt it for humans, which won't take much fine-tuning, we could in effect drop it on an enemy country; once the population turned, they would kill each other, and the rest would soon die of starvation, killing the virus at the same time. Just think: no longer would our soldiers have to go in on the ground and fight hand-to-hand; we could simply infect the water supply or the grain supply of a country and our problems would be solved! I'll win the Nobel Prize for this! I'll be famous!

"But first I need to deduce how long the virus will be viable in its host and how long it will take to infect said host. So much to do and so little time." The man started to giggle. Then the screen went black.

"Holy shit, that guys a modern day Dr. Frankenstein," Bill said. "That dumb bastard did this to all of us—he killed us all." He looked at the ID badge still in his hand and read the name on it again: Dr. Theodore Donaldson. The same face stared back at him from the small picture on the front of the badge.

Bill flicked the card away from him, disgusted. "Well, at least the bastard got a taste of his own medicine." He pushed himself off the desk and started for the door. "Come on, let's get back to the others and see what they've found."

Marie stood up and turned off the monitor out of habit, then followed Bill and Tessa.

"What do we tell the others?" Tessa asked him. "Do we tell them about the video?"

He shook his head, his face like stone. "They don't need to know what we found. Shit, if I could go back in time a few minutes, I would never have watched that damn video." He looked at the other two women, making sure they were on-board. "Do you agree with me? We keep what we know to ourselves."

Marie nodded, and after a moment so did Tessa.

"Good. Trust me, it's for the best. The others have enough to worry about." He turned to look at Tessa. "Sorry, honey, guess there wasn't any help here after all. It was a good try though."

She smiled wanly and the three survivors moved through the airlock.

CHAPTER 15

Back in the breakroom, Bill was pleased to see everyone had returned safely. Only Melissa was missing, still on watch near the front door. The others were now wearing fresh clothes.

Bill, Marie and Tessa quickly put on some for themselves, and though still dirty and sweating from their escape down the highway, it felt good to be wearing clothing again.

Bill chose a long-sleeve, button-down shirt that was about his size. Marie had on a New York Yankees polo shirt, which caused Bill to smile. Tessa went out in the hallway for privacy and changed into a yellow t-shirt and a pair of faded jeans that fit as if they were made for her.

Marie turned around in a circle, modeling her new wardrobe. "What, you don't like it?" she asked, noticing Bill's expression.

"No, Marie, you look fine." He looked at the other people around him. "Can someone relieve Melissa for a while, maybe for an hour or so? Then I'll come and do my shift."

"I'll go, Bill," Bruce said, raising his hand casually. "I could use some time to think about everything's that happened." He looked to Elizabeth and took her hand in his. "You okay?"

She nodded. "Sure, I'm fine. Go ahead. I'm sure Melissa wants to know what's happening, too."

Bruce squeezed her hand and then he was off, giving Bill a slight smile as he left.

Bill nodded, silently thanking him for relieving Melissa, and then he sat down at the table and slapped the tabletop, calling everyone to attention.

"All right then, so what did you guys find? Something useful, I hope."

Elizabeth, beaming with pride, pulled her hand from under the table and tossed Bill a box that rattled as it slid across the smooth Formica top. "How's this? I think they're the right size."

Bill picked up the box and turned it in his hands.

"Well I'll be damned. Bullets." He shook the box, rattling the contents. "And almost full, too." He pulled the .38 from his pants and quickly reloaded it, shaking out the spent casings.

Once he was finished, he spun the cylinder and cocked the weapon. "Damn, that feels good. I was out, you know; the damn gun was good for nothing but a club." He smiled at Elizabeth. "Thanks, you just might have saved us all."

She turned beet red, blushing. "Just glad to help," she said. "There were a few other boxes in one of the desks, but I was pretty sure they weren't the right size for your gun, so I only brought these with me."

"That's too bad—the more the better—but this is better than nothing. What we really need to do is find some more firearms."

"Did you guys find anything we could use?" Janice asked Bill and Marie.

"Not really," Bill said, giving Marie and Tessa a covert glance. "Just a room full of dead animals."

Everyone looked up when Melissa walked into the room, and Bill did too, glad for the distraction.

"How's it going out there, honey?" Marie asked.

Melissa grabbed a small bag of potato chips from the counter and started eating them as she dropped down in the seat Bruce had left. "Not so good. They just keep banging on the door. The damn hinges are going to bend soon." She looked at all the faces around her, and though she hated to say it, she did. "We need to get out of here before they break in, 'cause once they do, that's it—game over."

"Damn, what are we going to do?" Marie asked.

"That's not the worst of it," Elizabeth said. "When Bruce and I were checking out the other rooms, we were able to see out the windows. There's more of them showing up every second. We're surrounded. If we try to sneak out the back or out a window, they'll just see us and run us down."

"Great, that makes things even worse than when we were on the school," Bill said, squeezing his right hand into a fist. "At least there they couldn't get at us. But when we leave here, where do we go? There has to be someplace secure from those bastards."

"What about the camp we talked about earlier?" Kenny asked; everyone looked at him, making him uncomfortable. "That's outside the city. Maybe we could go there?"

"Shut up, Kenny," Tessa snapped. "You know that's not an option!"

"Tessa," Bill said, "I know what you said earlier about the camp, but it might just be our only option."

Tessa shook her head. "No way, forget it, we can't go there. It's a bad idea, trust me. Kenny doesn't know what he's talking about."

"Why, honey? Why's it such a bad idea?" Marie asked. "Maybe they can be reasoned with. They're the Army, for God's sake. And we're American citizens."

Tessa sighed and glowered at Kenny. Then she sat a little taller and told them what she knew.

"Me and Kenny met a few other people a day before we found you. They'd come from the camp. There was a woman with them, maybe my mom's age, and she said the soldiers at the camp were shooting anything that gets near their perimeter, whether they're infected or not. They said there were people in the camp that were doing experiments on anyone who wasn't infected, like lab rats.

"But the thing that scared me the most was that the guy in charge is running the place like a small country. If he decides he doesn't want you around anymore, he snaps his fingers and makes you disappear."

"What do you mean by disappear?" Janice asked.

"I mean they bring you to the back of the camp where they've dug a big grave and they shoot you," Tessa explained. "When there's too many bodies in the hole, they set it on fire. The lady that told us this ... Carol was her name, wasn't it Kenny?"

He nodded.

"Yeah, well, Carol said you could smell the bodies burning day and night. She said the smell got into your clothes so you couldn't get rid of it."

"Tell them what else she said, Tessa," Kenny said. "They might as well know."

Tessa nodded. "Well, she said the guy in charge is using people for slave labor, too. And if you don't agree with what he does, then he sends you to the back of the camp. Carol and her friends were lucky enough to sneak out, though some of them didn't make it."

"That doesn't sound like a place I'd like to visit," Marie said.

Nods and grunts of agreement filled the room.

Bill waved his hand, as if he could dismiss what he'd heard. "It all doesn't really matter, anyway. The first thing is to get out of here before that door gives out. Any suggestions on how we're going to do that?"

Everyone sat quiet, trying to think of how to get out of the building in one piece. No one had any ideas.

"I think I have an idea," Roger said from the corner of the room, finally speaking up. Since Bill had returned with Tessa and Marie, he'd merely sat quietly, watching and listening to the adults talk. "That is, if you'll listen to a kid."

Bill chuckled a little, glad to see the boy joining in on the discussion. "Hell, Roger, I'd listen to anyone at this moment; I'm not proud. What do you got?"

Roger smiled, his eyes creasing a little. He wasn't used to people taking him seriously, especially adults. Pushing out his chest, he moved to the table and leaned against it with his hands. He slipped Tessa a quick look, and she smiled, looked down at her sneakers. He smiled, too, then turned to face Bill and the others.

"Well, I think we need another distraction, like when we were on the roof of the school. Something so big those nutjobs out there will be too busy to worry about us."

Marie nodded, listening quietly. "Okay, honey, what do you have in mind?"

Roger grinned the same way a teenager does when he knows he's doing something bad, but it's far too much fun to worry about the consequences.

"What do you guys know about making pipe bombs?"

CHAPTER 16

"Pipe bombs?" Bill asked. "Are you serious?"

Roger nodded, took a deep breath. "It's not that hard, really. I used to go on the Internet and search all kinds of stuff. All you have to do is Google 'pipe bombs' and there's whole instructions on how to make them and use them."

"And you did this?" Marie asked.

Roger nodded. "Yup, sure did. I mean, it's not like I would have or anything, but it's cool to know how."

"So what do we do with them, use them like grenades?" Elizabeth asked.

Roger shook his head. "Well, sort of. We can put stuff in them like glass and nails. Thumbtacks would probably work pretty well, too. But they don't work exactly like grenades. They're pretty unstable. If you don't know what you're doing, then—boom!" He used his hands to pantomime a big explosion.

Bill leaned forward in his chair, his forehead wrinkling as he thought it over.

"Damn, Roger, that's not a half-bad idea. But what would we use for explosives?"

"That's the easy part. Elizabeth said there were more boxes of ammo in one of the desks, right? We can open the bullets and use the gunpowder."

"But won't we need a lot of them?" Melissa asked. "I mean, there's dozens of people outside. How will we be able to get everyone before they manage to rip us apart?"

"She's got a point," Janice added. "The second we open that door, or they bust it in, we'll be overwhelmed."

Everyone started talking at once, trying to talk over one another, throwing out ideas and concerns.

Phillip moved closer to Marie, not liking where the conversations were going. Marie held him close, telling him everything would be fine. She handed him a piece of the cookie she'd been munching on, and the boy ate it hungrily.

Bill held up his hands. "All right, enough!" he said over the group. "One at a time!"

Roger said, "We can do this, Bill, I promise. Besides, you got any better ideas?"

Tessa smiled, seeing that Roger was in control of the argument. "He's got a point, Bill, and we're short on time."

Bill sighed and slumped in his chair. "So what do we need to get this done?"

Roger smiled. "All right, excellent, okay, this is what we need ..."

Thirty minutes later, Bill walked to the front door of the building to check on Bruce, who was leaning against the two desks, using his body as added weight to keep the door closed.

"Hey, Bruce, how's it going out here?"

"So far, so good. But I don't think we have much time left." He pointed to the hinges and top lip of the door. "If you look closer, you can see where the paint's chipping as the metal bends. Please tell me you have a plan for getting us the hell out of here."

Bill grinned. "As a matter of fact, that's exactly what we're doing now. Elizabeth is coming to relieve you in a few minutes; what do you say you help out?"

"Sure, of course, whatever you need."

The two talked for a few minutes, making idle chatter. Bill found out Bruce was a lawyer with an office in the Loop, the historical part of Chicago. He mostly took civil cases, sometimes criminal cases if they weren't too serious.

He was just about ready to start talking about his wife when Elizabeth popped up. "You ready for a break, Bruce?"

"Sure am." He looked to Bill and smiled shyly. "Ah, Bill, why don't you go ahead of me and I'll catch up."

"Oh sure," he said, embarrassed. "No problem. First room on the right, at the end of the hall."

Elizabeth waved slightly as he walked away, turning to talk to Bruce as soon as he was gone.

Bill paused halfway down the hallway. In the wan light coming through a few side windows, he could see Bruce and Elizabeth, just two silhouettes coming together in an embrace. He grinned, happy for the both of them. It was good to see at least the two of them enjoying what happiness they could find.

A loud bang on the front door caused him to jump, the echo reverberating off the tile walls.

Turning, he moved off, walking a little faster now. He took a quick detour by the men's room to take care of some business, then headed for the room where the other survivors had gathered with the bomb supplies. Roger had suggested they use a large space to assemble the pipe bombs, so there would be distance from each person in case of an explosion. They had agreed to meet in the first large room they'd investigated, the cubicles perfect for isolating each worker.

The first thing Bill saw when he entered the office was that Roger was firmly in charge. The boy moved from table to table, showing each survivor how to assemble a pipe bomb.

Bruce had already arrived and was at a corner desk, prying open bullets, while a few desks over, Janice was drilling holes in the middle of six-inch water pipes with a drill.

Roger moved up to Bill, grinning from ear to ear. Bill pointed to Janice and asked about what she was doing.

"She drills a small hole in the middle and then we use a shoelace for a fuse," Roger explained, picking up a nearby pipe to demonstrate. "Once the pipe's full of gunpowder and you light the fuse ... well, you know the rest."

Bill looked over to see Marie carrying a handful of nails. "What're those for?"

"Makes 'em deadlier," Roger said proudly. "With nails and glass inside, the bomb'll cut anything around it to pieces."

"Where'd everybody find this stuff?"

"Well, there was a maintenance closet that had the tools and nails, and Bruce took apart some plumbing in one of the bathrooms downstairs. Then we got lucky and found the pipe caps in another closet with supplies and light bulbs and stuff. That's why pipe bombs are so cool: if you have something explosive to put in them, then the rest is all household items. In fact, if we didn't have gunpowder, we probably could have made due with a bunch of matchbook heads."

"So you learned all this on the Internet?" Bill asked.

"Yup, you can find out how to build anything—but you have to be careful. Google the wrong site and the Feds will be on your ass. That happened to a friend of mine."

Bill nodded, not really caring about some wild kid with too much time on his hands. "Um, listen, what can I do to help?"

Roger pointed to two more boxes of bullets. "You can open those up, but be careful."

"Sure, okay."

In less than half an hour all the items were ready to be assembled. But before they began, Roger stopped everyone.

"Now this is when it gets tricky. First, put the bottom cap on the pipe, and then the gunpowder goes in. Put a piece of tape on the fuse hole so nothing falls out. Once the powder's in—

and make sure to pack it almost near the top—put the nails inside. But be very careful. One spark and the powder can ignite, and that's bad."

"Ya think?" Bruce asked, clearly nervous.

"Bill, I think we should get the kids out of here," Marie suggested.

"You're right. Tessa, will you take Phillip and Kenny out into the hall? We'll tell you when it's safe to come back in."

"But I want to help," Tessa said.

"You will be helping if you look after Phillip. Please?" Bill tried to sound sincere.

Tessa sighed. "Come on, little man, let's go to the break-room. I think there's some cookies left. You too, Kenny, let's go."

Phillip grinned and ran out the door, with Tessa right behind him. She shot Bill a look that said she wasn't happy. Bill smiled and said "thank you" softly as she passed.

Kenny followed them out, his hands deep in his pockets.

With the kids gone, the others got to work. Bill started assembling his bomb, already blinking sweat out of his eyes. If he made one critical mistake, he would be nothing but a red stain on the ceiling.

He had to wonder if the homemade grenades would be enough. The more he thought about it, the more he realized they needed a much larger bang.

Then he remembered the hydrogen and oxygen tanks in the lab with all the deceased animals. If they attached the pipe bombs to those tanks and set them off just as the mob outside charged into the building, the massive explosion should take them all out, especially if he turned on the gas stove in the breakroom. The only question was, would the survivors be able to make it out before they were overwhelmed?

Pouring gunpowder into the pipe, he decided that problem could wait until he was done. He was packing the pipe with glass from a shattered soda bottle, and if what Roger said was true about sparks, then he wasn't looking forward to it.

Bruce, at the back of the room, didn't understand what the fuss was about; the nails went in easily enough, and then all he had to do was tighten the top cap.

With an adjustable wrench, he started to screw the top onto his second bomb. He turned the cap a little too fast, causing a small spark.

Bill happened to be looking over at him, checking on him and the others, trying to gauge how fast everyone was working compared to him.

Bruce disappeared in a blinding flash.

Janice, sitting nearby, was thrown off her chair; she fell to the floor in a heap of arms and legs.

Everyone started screaming, deafened by the explosion. Bill jumped to his feet, felt a wet spot on his cheek. When he wiped it away, he realized it was a piece of Bruce.

Marie had known enough to fall to the floor, which had probably saved her life. Bill stumbled around his desk, feeling lightheaded, and helped her to her feet.

"Are you okay?" he asked, brushing her hair from her face.

She nodded and pushed him away. Melissa was unscathed and was already moving to help her. "I'm fine. Go see to the others."

Bill did as she told him, reaching Roger next. The boy lay flat on his back, moaning. Shrapnel from the bomb had peppered his face with small cuts, but luckily he'd been far enough away to avoid the big pieces.

Bill helped him to a sitting position, and Roger held a hand to his head, wincing. "Oh wow, what happened?"

"I don't really know. One moment Bruce was sitting there working, the next he was just ... gone."

Roger shook his head. "Oh shit, I told you the stuff is unstable; you've got to move slowly. The poor bastard blew himself up!" He was yelling but didn't realize it, his ears damaged from the explosion.

Bill only heard the gist of it, deaf himself. Once he determined Roger was okay, he hobbled over to Janice.

She wasn't moving so he picked her up and held her. She had a gash on her forehead and a small amount of blood seeped through her shirt, but her chest was rising and falling; she was alive.

Bill situated her better in his arms, then left the smoke-filled room. Tessa was already in the hallway, her face filled with fear. She followed Bill into the breakroom, where he laid Janice down on a table.

"What happened?" Tessa asked. "Are we under attack? Did the crazy people get in? Are we in trouble?"

"Slow down, Tessa, give me a second."

Elizabeth ran into the breakroom, her eyes wide. She took one look at Janice and let out a small screech.

"Oh my God, what happened? It sounded like we're being attacked."

"One of the bombs went off," Bill explained, wringing out a rag in the sink before washing Janice's face with it. "She was caught in the blast."

"Oh God, no. Was anyone else hurt?"

Bill decided now was not the time to tell Elizabeth that Bruce was dead. He focused on Janice. "Help me with her, will you? I think her shoulder's bleeding."

While Tessa and Elizabeth held Janice steady, Bill removed her shirt, leaving the woman topless except for her bra. Her right shoulder had a piece of shrapnel in it, and Bill pulled out the metal shard and dropped it to the floor in one fluid motion. He placed the wet rag on the wound and wiped away most of the blood, relieved to see only a small gash. Tessa wiped Janice's forehead; the wound there was bloody, but not serious. All in all, she was lucky considering how close she'd been to the blast.

Bill bandaged her up and left her with Tessa and Elizabeth, then ran back to the office to see if he could help.

The room smelled like blood and smoke, and the explosion had left a black spot in the corner. Bruce's desk had shattered everywhere, adding splinters to the mess. The only good thing was the blast had been localized to his corner, keeping the other pipe bombs safe.

Marie and Melissa were standing, still shaken, finding it hard to believe they had just lost one of their own.

Roger was already gathering what could be used from Janice's desk, knowing that they still had to keep going. Bill nodded as he watched the teen working. The boy was regaining his confidence, realizing he was an asset to the group.

All eyes turned to Bill. He had nothing to say to them— what could he say?

He turned to the sound of slapping feet and saw Elizabeth standing in the door. Her eyes were wide as she looked from face to face.

"Where's Bruce? Why isn't he here? What the hell happened in here?"

Bill sighed, realizing he had to tell her. Elizabeth stepped into the room, and she saw the blackened desk and wall, the blood dripping from the ceiling. She shook her head, slowly at first, but then faster and faster as tears flowed down her cheeks.

"No, no, it's not true, he's not dead, he's fine." She stared at each face in the room, one at a time. "He's fine!" she screamed, her chest heaving as she tried to hold back the sobs.

Bill took her in his arms and held her tight. She fought him at first, shaking her head in disbelief.

"No, he's fine, he's okay!"

Bill hugged her, not letting her go. "I wish he was, God I do, but I'm so sorry, he's gone."

She struggled for a few more seconds as the words sank in. Then she went limp in his arms and sagged to the floor, crying. Bill let her go, gently easing her down.

Marie and Melissa both knelt down and hugged their friend.

Bill's heart felt like a lead weight. He'd seen the way Bruce and Elizabeth had looked at each other. They had found each other in a world turned upside down. And now it was all gone.

While Elizabeth sobbed on the floor, her shoulders shaking, Bill let one tear roll down his cheek. The tear was for many things. For his wife, now gone and buried. For Bruce and Elizabeth, a love that would never flourish. And most of all for the rest of them, still alive and fighting for an uncertain future.

He knelt down and hugged Marie and Melissa while the others held on to each other, hands squeezing as tears flowed.

It wouldn't last.

Even in their grief, they knew they had no time for mourning, but for just a moment everyone needed to be held, needed to know they weren't alone ... at least, not yet.

CHAPTER 17

Mike gazed out over what was once the city of Chicago, home to over three million people, now nothing but flaming buildings, some like giant torches burning in the falling dusk. The winds which gave the city its nickname spread the flames from structure to structure, the heat melting glass and steel. Pieces of the Aon Center fell to the street below, the sounds of destruction too far away for him to hear. Dean had been true to his word. Using tanker trucks full of gasoline and setting gas stations and propane refueling stations on fire, he had turned all of Chicago into Hell on Earth.

Mike looked over to where the Loop once stood, and all he could see was large black pillars of smoke and soot, the old buildings like kindling for the flames. The Sears tower had fallen almost an hour ago, the blaze finally hot enough to melt some of the steel frame. Now all that remained was a charred structure of molten steel and rubble.

The parks were ablaze as well, the lack of rain in the past few weeks contributing to the inferno. Rogers Park, Lincoln

Park, Jefferson Park and countless others burned brightly, the conflagration spreading with the wind.

With everything burning, all the survivors had tried to evacuate the city. Survivors who'd been hiding inside apartments, store basements and the back rooms of warehouses had no choice but to run for their lives. The Changed were waiting for them. One at a time, the people were taken down and slaughtered, torn apart by teeth and hands until there was no one left. Dean had managed to save a few as play toys, and Mike's stomach still rolled when he thought about what Dean had done to them. He felt even more nauseous when he thought about how he could have joined them if he hadn't bargained for his life. Though with Dean's grasp on reality, tenuous at best, he had no real idea for how long their deal would last.

Now Mike had to lead Dean to Bill and the others, and the scary thing was he didn't exactly know where they'd gone. He could only hope to stall Dean long enough to figure a way out of this horrible mess he'd gotten himself into before he became another bloody heap on the ground.

Dean came up behind him and slapped him on the back. The man smiled, his teeth red with blood from a young woman he'd just finished torturing, raping and killing. Her screams still echoed in Mike's ears.

"What's the matter, Mikey, my boy? Feeling blue?" When he was in a good mood, Dean had begun calling him Mikey. The only problem was, if Dean was in a good mood that probably meant he'd just killed someone.

"No, I'm fine, just thinking about stuff."

"What the hell's there to think about? The world is over, nothing to think about now but how to enjoy what's left." He scratched his nose with his finger, leaving a bloody smear on his skin. "Look, we're leaving in a few minutes, and you're on point. I want you to lead me straight to the others you told me about."

Mike turned around to look at Dean and tried to control his disgust. Dean was covered in blood; only his face was relatively clean.

"What if I can't find them? What if they've moved on?"

Dean smiled, his stained teeth flashing. "Well, then, Mikey, old chum of mine, I guess I won't need you anymore and I can give you to *them*." He pointed over his shoulder to the monstrous crowd of infected.

Mike's stomach jumped into his throat. Thousands of men, women, and children, filled the street, their bodies disappearing around the corner at the intersection a block away. Every infected person in the city was now standing behind them.

"Oh my God," Mike gasped, watching the shifting crowd of people, some of them barely old enough to walk.

"God had nothing to do with it, Mike, my boy. I'm God now, and with your help I'll lead the Changed across this nation. My wrath will be swift." Dean looked at Mike. "What's wrong? Go ahead, you can tell me. I won't kill you ..."

Mike couldn't stop himself even if he wanted to; the words needed to come out, even if it was just so he could hear them with his own ears. "You're fucking crazy, you're absolutely insane."

Dean chuckled and turned to the giant crowd, his subjects. "This man says I'm crazy! Am I?"

As one large entity, the crowd roared and pumped their hands, the nearby glass in the second-story buildings shaking from the ferocity of their screams.

Dean turned back to look at Mike, his eyes alight with excitement. "Do you remember the old saying, 'If you can't beat 'em, then join 'em'?"

Mike nodded slightly.

"Good. Because we are the new world, and if you don't become one of us, then there's no need to keep you around." He turned to his people once again, raising his hands in the air, and they yelled and cheered. The crowd wanted something to kill, anything, and Mike had never felt so vulnerable.

Dean flashed Mike a sly grin. "Don't worry, Mikey. I said I wouldn't kill you and I meant it. As long as you help me, I'll let you keep breathing." Mike thought he was done, but then Dean added one more tidbit. "However long that might be." Then he walked away to prepare his people for evacuation.

They had all gathered near the city limits, the clothing store where Mike had met Dean now reduced to cinders. The inferno was spreading quickly, and if Dean didn't leave soon, he and his followers would burn.

Darkness was falling fast, thanks to the ash-filled sky, but Dean didn't seem to mind. What did he have to fear?

He was the predator, the dominant species. He was at the top of the food chain.

Mike turned away from the massive crowd and concentrated on the flames as they slowly consumed the city.

Chicago was dead, nothing but ashes, and Mike knew if he didn't figure out what to do soon, he, too, would be dead.

CHAPTER 18

After Bruce's death, the pipe bomb assembly went slowly for a while as everyone tried to adjust to the loss. It went even slower because they were taking the utmost care with the explosives. As Bill finished tightening the cap on his last bomb, he cringed, just waiting for the spark. Luck was with him and the cap went on easily. He laid the wrench down and let out a sigh that the entire room heard, despite that they had pushed their desks farther apart to minimize damage in case of another blast.

Roger took up the slack after Bruce's death; he seemed to have a knack for building the small explosives.

"Are you sure you never did this before?" Bill had asked while Roger was helping him with the second bomb.

Roger had nodded. "Bill, I swear, I only read about them online. I never actually did anything. I mean, look at this face; I'm too pretty to go to jail."

Bill stacked his last device with the others lying neatly on the desk, each with a piece of shoelace sticking out the side. He looked over his shoulder at the others. Melissa was almost finished, her red hair plastered with sweat against her face.

Elizabeth was back on door duty, too fraught with loss to help make bombs. She had been almost catatonic after they lost Bruce, and though Bill had known the two were close, he'd had no idea just how close.

Janice was still in the breakroom with Tessa, Kenny and Phillip. She'd regained consciousness a little while after the explosion and would be ready to go when it came time to escape. Bill figured they'd spring the trap in an hour or so, right after nightfall.

Marie was working on her second bomb, and Bill decided to help her. He walked over and smiled, almost tiptoeing across the floor. "How's it going?" he asked softly. "Need any help?"

She didn't hear him at first, concentrating on packing her pipe with nails and shards of glass. Bill waited patiently while she finished. Once the last of the glass was in the pipe, she let out a loud sigh. Her arms glistened with sweat.

"Hey," she said, drying her brow, suddenly realizing Bill was beside her. "Didn't see you there, sorry. I was a little preoccupied."

"Want any help?"

She shook her head. "No, I'm okay. Why don't you do something else if you're done with yours?"

"Okay then, I'll go get the tanks from the lab; that'll be the icing on the cake. Be careful, all right?"

"I'll be nothing but. You watch yourself, too."

He waved bye and walked into the hall to retrieve the hydrogen and oxygen tanks from the lab.

Glancing over his shoulder, he saw Elizabeth's legs as she sat on the tile near the front door at the opposite end of the hallway. Though the banging sounds had slowed a little, the mob outside still made plenty of noise. Bill debated going to check on her, make sure she was all right, but he decided to leave her alone. Hopefully, she could come to grips with Bruce's death and be ready to leave when the time came.

In the lab, Bill walked down the center aisle between the cages, staring at some of the animal carcasses. He had always had a soft spot for animals, and his late wife Laura had always teased him that he had a heart of gold.

Using a dolly he found in the corner, Bill transported the hydrogen and oxygen tanks back to the hallway. He'd even been fortunate enough to find a small propane tank used to fuel the Bunsen burners. Though the gauge had read only half full, he was sure it would only add to the blast.

Feeling good to have a task that wouldn't blow him up at a second's notice, he quickly moved each tank out of the lab and found himself whistling, just happy to be doing a mundane task in a world gone psychotic.

Elizabeth sat on the floor and watched the front door shake in its frame.

Her heart ached terribly when she thought about Bruce. God, she missed him. Though they'd only been together for a short time, she had grown to love the man.

She wanted to just stand up, push the desks out of the way, and unlock the door, letting in the ravenous mob. It would only hurt for a moment before death took her into its warm embrace.

Tears flowed down her cheeks again as the pain of loss filled her.

She let it out and continued to stare at the door, knowing in time she would have the strength to end it once and for all. And when she did, she knew Bruce would be waiting for her in Heaven.

When Bill was satisfied with the position of the tanks in the hall, he went back to the large office space to see how the others were fairing.

"Good timing, Bill," Roger said, grinning from ear to ear. "We just finished." Bill walked over to the table in the middle of the room where they had stacked all the pipe bombs. There were nine in all, minus the three Bruce would have made.

Marie moved next to him, her breath coming in short gasps. "Frightening, isn't it, to think we actually made bombs?"

Bill nodded. "New world, different rules. Not only did we build them, but we're about to use them to kill hundreds of people."

"Perhaps. But if we don't, those same people will be happy to tear us apart."

"True," he replied.

"So, what's next?" Melissa asked, leaning against a nearby desk.

Bill and Roger had already discussed using the bombs in tandem with the gas tanks, and now Bill turned and squeezed the boy's shoulder like a father to a son.

"We make those tiny bombs into big ones, and hopefully get the hell out of here," Bill said to them all.

Marie pulled Melissa toward the doorway. "All right then, let's get started. Time's a wasting, boys."

Bill and Roger did as they were told, gathering up the makeshift bombs and a roll of duct tape; they followed Marie out into the corridor, walking as if they were carrying dynamite, which wasn't far from the truth.

The sun was almost down, and when it finally set they needed to be ready to move. But there was still a lot to accomplish and not a lot of time to get it done.

CHAPTER 17

Bill's idea was simple and straightforward. Strap the pipe bombs to the hydrogen and oxygen tanks and place them in the middle of the corridors against the support columns of the building. Then, while the rampaging crowd poured through the front door and into the long hallway, Bill would light the fuses and hightail it to the door at the far end. If things went as planned, almost the entire crowd of raving lunatics would be inside the building when the explosions brought the structure down.

In the ensuing chaos, the group of survivors could slip into the darkness and with luck find a car or some kind of transport. As to where to go after that ... well, Bill hadn't figured that out yet. Better to see if they lived through the first part of the plan before worrying about the second; after all, there were a whole lot of hopefully's to get through before the plan was a success.

Roger and Bill taped the bombs to the tanks while the others fidgeted, wanting only to help.

Bill saw this and nodded to Marie. "This is a two-man job. Why don't you collect any food left in the breakroom, and when you're done bring Tessa and the others with you. We're almost ready to do this."

He turned to Melissa, who was fidgeting in the corner. "Why don't you go help, too?"

Both women agreed and quickly left, feeling good to have something to do. When they were gone, Roger spoke up, securing the last bomb to one of the tanks.

"You really think this'll work?" he asked, looking at the tanks spread out across the main hall. Each one was set near a support column. While Bill was no engineer, he knew enough about construction and demolition, thanks to reading a lot and asking questions on job sites where buildings were being demolished. Usually the demolition experts were happy to share their knowledge, enjoying a captive audience. Almost everyone Bill had ever met was happy to talk about their job or personal life.

He wiped the sweat from his brow and finished securing the final pipe bomb to an oxygen tank. He had positioned it between the other hydrogen tanks, hoping the different size explosions would complement each other.

The propane tank was in the middle of the hallway, where he hoped it would do the most damage.

Bill joined Roger in the middle of the hall. "Honestly, I have no idea if it'll work, but it sure beats waiting to be slaughtered when they finally break in here. At least this way we're still fighting."

"I guess that's all we can do," Roger said quietly.

Bill rubbed the boy's shoulder. "If it helps you feel better, I can lie and tell you everything's gonna be fine."

Roger shook his head. "Nah, I hate being bullshitted. Just tell me like it is and I'll deal with it."

Bill grinned. "Spoken like a true warrior. Come on, let's get this party started. It's dark outside, so there's no more reason to stay here." They headed to the end of the hallway to meet up with the others.

Marie and Melissa were just coming around the corner, carrying Janice between them. Though she said she could walk herself, the other two women insisted on at least half-carrying her. Tessa, Kenny and Phillip were right behind them.

Bill looked at their haggard faces and realized how their group continued to shrink. He could only hope they had the same number of people when they finally put this place behind them.

He clapped his hands while they approached, smiling sincerely. "Fantastic, ladies and gentleman. You guys get to the rear entrance and I'll go get Elizabeth. Roger, seems you've got a lighter, so I guess you're on fuse duty. Unless you want me to do it."

"No way, man. All this was my idea in the first place; it should be me who lights them. Besides, if the shoelaces don't take, I'll have to set them off manually with a hammer."

"You're not serious, are you?" Janice asked, leaning on Marie for support, her voice weak but growing stronger with each minute.

Roger nodded. "Damn straight. If those bombs don't go off, then this is all for nothing."

Marie held up a hand to calm the others. "Relax everyone, it won't come to that, I promise. You'll see in a few minutes, we'll all be away from here and on our way to someplace safe."

Though no one believed her, Marie's soothing voice put the others at ease.

Bill handed Roger one of the two-way radios they'd found in an office. He assumed the radios were used for drills or something similar. Now they were crucial to the plan. After Bill retrieved Elizabeth and unlocked the front door, he believed it would only be seconds before the infected mob stormed inside. Roger would need time to light the fuses and then evacuate with the others.

With Elizabeth in tow, Bill hoped to race past the burning fuses and out the rear door just before the bombs went off.

"All right then, Roger, be ready. I'll be calling you in a few minutes and then light 'em up." With a brief wave, he took off down the hallway, his adrenaline already pumping.

Roger watched him go. "Now all we have to do is wait for Elizabeth and Bill, then it's show time," he said, trying to psych himself up for the task ahead.

Bill moved swiftly down the hallway, closer to the banging on the front door. The windows of Star Labs had been covered in metal lattice for security, which had kept out the infected. Now the same safety feature hindered their escape. The only way out of the building was the rear exit, and Bill could only hope once the crazies realized the front door was open, they would all quickly abandon the rear entrance and join their fellow brethren in the front.

As Bill approached the door, he immediately noticed the top desk had been shoved off to the side. He pulled his .38 revolver from his waistband. He had six rounds in the weapon and more in his pocket, though he doubted he'd have time to reload once all hell broke loose.

Elizabeth was already pushing the bottom desk away from the shaking door.

Bill ran toward her. "Elizabeth, what the hell are you doing? We're not ready yet—stop!"

She turned to look at him and Bill saw the bloodshot eyes and wet cheeks.

"Screw you, Bill, and screw everything. I'm sick of this shit. Bruce is gone and we'll be next. What the hell is the point?"

Bill stopped and held up his hand. "Hey now," he said.

Elizabeth paused. He could tell by the look in her eyes she was still not sure about committing suicide.

"Now, Liz ... can I call you Liz? You're just distraught about Bruce and everything else that's happened, and who could blame you? Just come over here and I promise everything will be fine."

Elizabeth gestured to the gun in Bill's hand. "Fine, huh? If everything's so damn fine, why do you have a gun? No, Bill, nothing's fine and it'll never be fine again. You can keep fighting if you want, but I give up!" She turned, pushed the desk out of the way and unlocked the door in one quick, almost practiced motion.

"Don't!" Bill shouted, taking two more steps toward her, but as the door opened and bloody hands shot through the crack, he started backpedaling.

It was too late for her. The crazies pulled her through the door, and her screams filled the hallway.

"Roger, we've got a problem," Bill called into the radio as he ran back down the hall. "Light the damn fuses right now and get the hell out of there!"

"What, now?" Roger asked, his voice crackling. "But I'm not ready."

"Well, I'm coming whether you're ready or not, so get moving or we're all dead." Just before he turned the corner at an intersection of the east and west hallways, he glanced over his shoulder to see how close the killers were.

All he saw was a mass of bodies filling the hallway and maybe a severed head bobbing above the crowd. As he turned the corner, he was almost positive it was Elizabeth's head, floating over the crowd like some kind of avenging angel.

For the next one and a half minutes, Bill ran through the long hallway until he turned the corner where Roger was lighting the fuses. He slid on the tile floor and kept moving, his motion too fast to stop him. "We've got to go!" he screamed. "They're right behind me!"

Roger lit another fuse and turned to Bill. "What the hell's going on? What happened to the plan?"

"No time—we've got to go!" He pulled Roger with him as he ran for the back door.

"But I'm not done yet—they won't blow up right!"

"Just run!"

Roger did run, but only a few feet, then he ripped his arm away from Bill and stopped moving.

"What are you doing? We need to go!"

The first of the infected rounded the corner.

"No," Roger said. "All the bombs need to go off at once; I didn't light them all. Just go and I'll make sure it happens!" He started running back toward the tanks that hadn't been lit.

"Damn it, Roger, no!" Bill screamed, though everything Roger had said made perfect sense.

"Just get out of here! If these don't blow, we're all dead! Tell Phillip I love him! Tell him what I did to save him!" He picked up a hammer from the floor as he went.

Bill hesitated for only a moment, realizing there was nothing he could do. In seconds the infected would be on top of him.

Cursing loud enough to echo down the hall, he turned and ran as fast as he could, leaving a boy to do a man's job.

Roger made it to the first tank as the infected crowd closed in. Hands reached out and pulled him down. He managed to kick the attacker away, but another one jumped at him. He only had to keep them off for a few seconds as Bill and the others made their escape. He used the hammer as a weapon, cracking skulls and caving in foreheads.

None of the infected ran past him, all seeking to kill him first.

A woman sank her teeth into his throat; a man bit into his leg. Roger screamed, his neck and shirt hot and wet with blood. He hit the woman with the hammer, smashing her left eye, bone and all, then kicked the man away from his leg.

His vision grew blurry and he realized it was now or never.

Pushing the crowd away, knowing he had less than a heartbeat, Roger swung the hammer at the pipe bomb just as the fuses on the other bombs burned down.

More attackers pounced on him, their hands and teeth sinking into his flesh. He screamed, but the pain was brief.

His last thoughts were of his little brother. He hadn't always treated him well, had always kicked Phillip out of his room and had never played games with him when he promised he would. He realized too late that his little brother only wanted to be with him because he loved him, and Roger had taken him for granted. Now he hoped he gave Phillip the ultimate gift: life, and maybe a way out of the crazy world he had been tossed into.

Then the bombs exploded and his lungs filled with fire; his face burned away from his skull.

The detonations rocked the building, shot flames through hallways and around corners. The shrieking mob was burned alive, and those that lived were killed when the structure collapsed.

Only a few seconds before the blast, Bill bolted down the corridor, knowing time was running out.

Marie was at the back door with the others, waiting for Bill, Elizabeth and Roger. She was surprised and shocked to hear Bill yelling from far away down the hall.

"What's he yelling about?" Tessa asked.

"No idea, honey, but we'll find out soon enough."

Bill rounded the bend, waving his hands in front of himself like one of the infected.

"Go, go! Open the damn door and get out of here—the bombs are going off any second!"

"Where's Roger and Elizabeth?" Melissa shouted, trying to see behind Bill.

"Just run, goddammit—hurry!"

Marie did as she was told and opened the rear door. The night air poured into the hallway, caressing her hair.

Bill ran into the doorframe, stopping sharply and breathing in quick gasps. "Get your asses moving!"

They scurried outside. Tessa and Kenny had to drag Phillip through the door as the boy hollered for his brother. Melissa slipped out behind them. No screams of pain—the coast was clear.

"What's happening?" Marie asked Bill. "Why are you alone?"

"Tell you later. Now for the love of God, run!" He pushed her in front of him as he lunged out of the building, looking back over his shoulder. Deep down inside he hoped to see Roger running around the corner, waving his hands in triumph, but he knew that wouldn't be happening.

When he heard the blast, he knew his time was up. He turned, preparing to run through the door and into the back parking lot. The blast deafened him, threw him into the air, his arms and legs flailing. He hit the pavement and managed to crawl a few more feet, hopefully out of the blast zone.

Then his vision faded and he passed out for a few seconds. When he opened his eyes again, the world around him was eerily quiet, as if all sound had been sucked up in the explosion.

Moaning, his eyes still closed, Bill flexed his hands and moved his legs, amazed that nothing was broken despite the pain. His senses flooded back to him, and he knew he needed to get up and see to the others. He'd heard nothing from any of them, and he started to worry.

Bill opened his eyes a little, wondering if any of their pursuers had survived the bombs. The night was filled with dust, smoke and residual explosions as the collapsed building settled.

Coughing hard on the grit, Bill rolled onto his back and looked up, expecting to see the night sky.

Instead, he saw a man standing over him. A man in a white biological containment suit and a military issue gas mask. The M-16 pointed at Bill's face was most definitely military issue.

Firelight from the destroyed building flooded the rear parking lot, creating a false dusk. But then night became day when three military troop carriers turned on their headlights, blinding him, making him close his eyes once more.

The man standing over him said, "Don't move! You're under arrest by the United States Army. If you so much as twitch one pinky, you will be shot." The gas mask muffled his voice, but not his authoritarian tone. Bill had no reason to doubt the faceless soldier.

"I'm not one of those killers," Bill said. "None of us are. We're not infected."

The soldier nodded, his rifle never wavering. "Maybe you're immune, or maybe you're just not showing signs yet. Either way, you're coming with us." He gestured with the muzzle of the rifle. Bill noticed his .38 was now jammed into the soldier's web belt; he must have dropped it when the explosion threw him.

Bill rolled to his feet, moaning, a thousand nerves flaring in pain. He was pushed toward the last transport and forced to board it, pleased to see his fellow survivors were all there, their frightened faces peering out of the shadows.

Every now and then they heard a gunshot as soldiers took down any murderous survivors from the explosion.

The soldier with the M-16 waved his hand to the other transports, giving the command to mount up. The dozen or so men spread around the perimeter did as ordered, and soon the truck was rumbling away, two soldiers with rifles keeping watch over the group. More gunshots sounded and screams joined the din as a few of the infected tried to attack the soldiers. Inside the truck, Bill couldn't see what was happening.

He sat next to Marie, holding onto a crossbeam as the truck jumped and rolled.

"Do you think we're saved? That they'll help us?" Marie asked with a spark of hope.

Bill looked at Melissa, Tessa and the others, then at Marie. He frowned, thinking back to what Tessa had said about the military camp.

"I'd like to think that's the case, but you know the saying 'Out of the frying pan and into the fire'?"

She and the others nodded.

"Well, something tells me we're just out of the pan."

"All of you, shut the fuck up or be shot," one of the soldiers said, the rifle bouncing in his hands as the truck rumbled onto the main road. Bill couldn't tell if it were the first soldier he'd seen. With their masks on, they all looked alike.

He decided to do as he was told and remain silent for the time being. He and his friends glanced at one another, trying to comfort each other with their eyes as the transport drove off into the night, their destination unknown.

CHAPTER 20

Dean called a halt when he saw the explosion across the highway. The darkness made it easy to spot the eruption of flames, and the noise of the collapsing building soon followed.

Dean cringed, sensing that a large group of his people had just perished. With every passing hour, he grew more attuned to his fellow Changed. He still didn't know why he was granted a consciousness while the others were nothing more than killing machines, but he knew he would use the power well.

Perhaps that was why the Changed listened to him with such devotion. They, too, sensed his greatness.

Thousands followed behind him, a flow of heads and shoulders. Some seemed to rise off the ground as they swarmed over an abandoned car or truck; there were too many bodies crowding the highway to go around the wrecks.

The fires in Chicago had forced them to migrate south toward the Midway International Airport, situated near the edge of Lake Michigan. Fortunately, Mike believed the other normals had journeyed in the same direction.

Two birds with one stone: one of his foster fathers had told him that saying. He'd been a drunk, the kind of guy who only set his bottle down long enough to beat his kid.

Dean pointed at the explosion, still burning less than a mile away. "Do you see that, Mikey? That was the normals you told me about, yes?"

Mike shrugged. "All I know is they were walking this way when I saw them, before I turned off the highway to go into the city. The biggest mistake of my life," he muttered.

Dean heard him anyway. "You think so? Actually, I think it was the best thing you could have done. If not for me, the Changed would have ripped you to pieces, so look at the bright side: even if I kill you, I can almost guarantee you'll be the last normal in the state of Illinois when I do."

"Some consolation."

Dean chuckled. "Well, I guess it's all a matter of opinion. Shall we continue? I'd like to see what survived that explosion." He didn't have high hopes of finding anything. Dean didn't know how, but he sensed the normals had been within his grasp, but that they had eluded him. The death of so many of his brethren only proved this assumption.

Before moving on, he turned to Mike and gazed into his eyes. "I warn you, Mike, if I even sense your prevarication, I'll kill you."

"My what? I don't understand what you just said."

Dean sighed, frustrated. "I said, you better not be telling me lies."

Mike swallowed a large lump in his throat and nodded quickly. "Oh, ah, understood."

"All right then, let's move out. There's a lot to investigate."

About twenty minutes later, Dean set his right foot down near the remains of Star Labs. The middle of the building had collapsed, bricks and rubble strewn everywhere, the parking lot illuminated by numerous small fires. Dean could make out arms and legs sticking out of the rubble at odd angles, and when he moved around the rear of the building, he spotted his first clue to what had happened here.

A soldier wearing a white suit lay on the black asphalt, his body covered by rubble, his head turned almost all the way around so that his back and his face were pressed to the concrete.

"You, you and you," Dean said, pointing to three of the Changed. "Dig him out. I want a better look at him."

The three men dove into the pile with gusto, tossing bricks and pieces of metal away from the corpse. Some of the flying debris struck other infected, who screamed when they were hit, but otherwise stood still. Dean rolled his eyes to the sky and asked, "Why me?"

In no time the body was clear. Dean kicked it. The dead soldier rolled over onto his stomach, his bloody face now staring at the sky.

"Soldiers," Dean said crisply. "I might have known." He turned to Mike and stuck his finger under the man's nose. "So help me, Mike, if you knew anything about this ..."

Mike held his hands in front of him. "Whoa there, Dean, I swear I don't know anything about this shit."

Dean stared at him, trying to discern whether or not he was lying. After a full minute he looked away.

"Fine, I guess it's not your fault. That's okay, though, because when I catch up to them, they will all die horribly."

Mike only nodded, too afraid to say anything.

Dean grunted, satisfied, and then pulled the closest Changed to him, a middle-aged woman with scraggly, light-brown hair. He needed females for the mission he had in mind. They wouldn't be as easily distracted by prey like the males would.

"You, gather a few other women and run ahead of us. At least three miles. Send one of you back to tell me what you find."

The woman grunted and ran off to do his bidding.

"Come along, Mikey," Dean said, starting back toward the highway with his troop. "There's a long road in front of us and a short time to get there."

Mike took one last look at the dead soldier and quickly ran after Dean.

CHAPTER 21

"Where's my brother?" Phillip asked from the front of the truck bed. One of the soldiers gave the boy a dirty look, but that's as far as the threat went. At least the soldiers had some decency left underneath their gas masks and bio-suits.

Bill looked to Marie for support. How could he tell a five-year-old boy his only living family member had just given his life to save them all? Marie shrugged.

Tessa spoke up. "Roger's not coming with us, Phillip. He's staying behind to help the soldiers. He'll be with us soon, though." She offered a false smile.

One of the soldiers growled at her and Tessa flipped him the finger. The soldier was about to stand up when the second soldier held his arm.

"Leave it alone, Bob. The sergeant major said he wanted them alive."

Bob cursed under his mask and sat back down. "Alive, yeah, but he didn't say we couldn't bruise them a little."

The first soldier shook his head, exasperated, the gesture barely noticeable under his containment gear.

"Look, Bob, do what you want, but don't blame me when you're on corpse duty."

That seemed to make Bob think for a second, and he realized maybe he was getting carried away. Tessa acted like she'd scored some kind of moral victory and stuck her tongue out at the conflicted soldier.

While Bob grumbled under his mask and tightened his grip on his rifle, the other soldier only chuckled.

Bill leaned forward so only Tessa could hear him. "It might be best not to agitate them, Tessa. At least not until we know what we're going into."

She just grinned and looked away, hugging Kenny with her left arm. The boy had been quiet since they had boarded the truck, intimidated by the alien-looking soldiers. Melissa and Janice sat near the opening of the bed, the wind blowing their hair around their faces. Both women were subdued, unable to grasp what had happened and why Elizabeth hadn't made it.

Bill didn't blame them. In only a few short hours they'd lost almost half their group. What would happen in another day, or a week, if the odds for survival were now this difficult?

"Where are you taking us?" Bill asked the soldiers. "We have a right to know."

"You have a right to shut the fuck up, unless you want to be spitting teeth," Bob said, sticking the rifle under Bill's chin.

Bill held up his hands. "All right, take it easy. It's just that we've been on the run for a while now, trying to stay ahead of those people out there. Actually, it's great to see you guys."

Soldier number two let out a loud sigh that Bill could hear through the man's gas mask. "Lighten up, Bob, they're just people." To Bill he said, "Though for the life of me I don't know why you're not infected."

Bill grinned slightly. "Just lucky I guess."

"Lucky my ass," Bob said. "If it wasn't for these masks I'd probably be one of those killers out there. I tell you, it ain't right why some people are fine and some ain't."

"So there are others like us?" Marie asked. "People that are okay?"

Soldier number two nodded slightly. "Some are immune, like you, though most people, once exposed, become crazy and lose all sense of who they are. If it wasn't for the sergeant-major realizing what was happening and making us put on masks, we'd probably be like the rest of them."

Bill nodded, glad to be getting some information. The more they could find out, the better off they'd be.

"So, may I ask where we're going, please?" he asked as politely as he could.

"All right, fine, might as well tell you. After all, once we get there you'll know anyway. We're going to Midway Airport."

"Midway Airport? Why?" Marie asked, keeping her tone as nice as possible. "Why not a military installation or some kind of refugee camp? I heard there was one nearby."

The soldier nodded. "Yup, there was one until more than five hundred infected people overran it. Luckily, we were already preparing to bug out, and almost all of us got out. It was the major's idea to set up at the airport. After all, they've already got fences and checkpoints, and the terminals make a great staging point for the doctors, the research staff, and the rest of our unit. Not to mention where you're going."

"Where are we going?" Bill inquired.

"To the isolation ward that's been set up," Bob said. Bill guessed the man was smiling under his gas mask, and he wanted nothing more than to lean over and pull it off his face, but what would that accomplish? Either the man would shoot him, or he would turn into a raving killer and attack.

Bill squeezed his hands into fists, holding his temper in check. "Isolation ward, why? If we're not sick, then we're not a threat to anyone."

The second soldier shrugged. "Look, pal, I'm just a grunt. I leave the thinking to the docs and my superiors. Now we're almost there, so how about piping down and letting me rest for a while, huh? I've been on duty for almost twenty-four hours straight."

Bill nodded, satisfied. Though some of the answers only brought more questions, he was smart enough to know when to stop pushing.

Beyond the rear of the truck bed, the city of Chicago faded away into the night. Smoke and fire filled the air, painting the horizon the color of blood.

The truck slowed to a stop almost an hour later and Bill realized he'd dozed off. Not surprising, really. In the last few days he'd spent so much time running and fighting, sleep had been the last thing on his mind. He felt like he was moving through molasses as he tried to shake the weariness from stiff limbs.

The soldiers jumped down to the tarmac where they were joined by three more men, all in white bio-containment suits and matching gas masks. Bill was the last to hop down out of the truck.

It was still dark, sunrise a few hours away, but it was easy to see where they were: an airport. Planes sat silent on the tarmac, waiting for another chance to reach the skies.

Bill wondered if they would ever leave the ground again. If the infection was as bad as it appeared to be, all the pilots were probably running around like rabid dogs.

"Move out toward the terminal," one of the soldiers ordered.

The survivors were herded like cattle across the open runway, soldiers flanking them on all sides.

"Kind of overkill for little old us, don't you think?" Marie commented dryly.

"I know what you mean," Melissa said. "What do they think we're gonna do? Without weapons they'd slaughter us."

One of the soldiers heard the conversation and stepped a little closer. "I know it seems like we're being too cautious, but after what happened at the camp, the sergeant-major's taking no chances. You'll see once you meet him." The soldier moved away then, afraid to be seen fraternizing with the prisoners. Still, it gave Bill hope that perhaps not all them were dangerous, that in fact some sympathized with their situation.

In less than five minutes, the terminal doors were in sight. Bill noticed some kind of tent on the other side and realized it was a pressurized air chamber, similar to the one they'd found at Star Labs, only this one was a temporary structure used by the CDC and other government authorities when airborne diseases were known to be prevalent.

One at a time, the group was ushered through the airlock and then down a ten foot tunnel lined with bright ultraviolet lights. The hair on Bill's face burned slightly as he passed through. When he stepped out the other side, he turned and waited for his friends. His skin felt slightly raw and he guessed the lights must have sterilized it, along with his clothing, destroying any bacteria that may have clung to him from the outside world. His clothes actually steamed slightly from the heat.

Fiver minutes later, the survivors were together once more, as were the soldiers. The soldier on Bill's right was the first to remove his mask, showing the blue eyes and smooth, pale chin of a young man, no older than eighteen or nineteen.

"Move along," the soldier said. "This way to the sergeant major." Bill was sure this was the soldier who had talked to him on the walk over, as the kindness in his eyes suggested. The other soldiers also removed their gas masks, revealing a wide assortment of men. Spanish, Black and Irish were just some of the nationalities represented. They all seemed relieved to be breathing the canned air.

Normally, thousands of people crowded the airport, all catching their planes or waiting on a layover, filling the terminal and the others connected to it by long walkways, which were now blocked off; the place was deserted. Bill moved through the terminal, noticing there were only a few soldiers moving about. All carried M-16 rifles and wore side arms on their hips; a few had small knives on their belts, too.

Bill slowed when they passed another temporary chamber. The doors were transparent, and men with lab coats moved about inside. Just before Bill was pushed away, he thought he saw a body on a table, but couldn't be sure.

"Marie, did you see that?" he asked softly, moving his head left and right to make sure one of the guards didn't catch him talking.

"See what?"

"Never mind, I'll tell you later."

After a few left turns and right turns and a trip up an escalator, Bill realized he was totally lost. They slowed as they approached a door labeled SECURITY.

One of the soldiers opened the door, and Bill and the others were ushered inside.

The room was huge, full of screens and computers. If Bill was right, this was the heart of airport security, a pretty good headquarters, he had to admit.

A man wearing a pair of BDU's and smoking a cigar walked over to the group, stopping three feet away, just at the edge of a one-foot platform. Bill and the rest of the group had no choice but to look up at him.

Psychologically speaking, it was a good ploy.

The young soldier with the kind eyes walked up to the front of the group, smiling as he gestured toward the man with the cigar.

"Ladies and gentlemen, I'd like to introduce you to our commander and savior, Sergeant Major Thaddeus Deckard."

With such an introduction, Bill wondered if he was supposed to clap. Instead, he stepped forward and held out his hand. "I'm Bill Thompson and I'm kind of the leader of our little group."

Deckard let out a puff of smoke and stared at Bill's hand as if deciding whether or not he should shake it. Bill was starting to feel stupid and was about to withdraw when the sergeant major stepped down from his platform and grasped Bill's hand. The handshake was nothing impressive and Bill was happy when the soldier let go. He had always found it unsettling when he shook another man's hand and the grip was weak. Said something about the character of the man shaking.

"Hello there, Mr. Thompson," Deckard said. "I just wanted to meet you before you were brought to containment. It's good we found you. Your country needs you ... all of you. For some reason, you people haven't been infected and we hope, nay pray, that there's something in your blood that will help us find a cure. So thank you in advance for cooperating and I hope to see you soon." He looked over at one of the soldiers, a large man with bright red hair and freckles. "Okay, Connelly, move them out."

"Yes, Sergeant Major." With their rifles aimed at Bill and the others, Connelly and the rest of the soldiers ushered the group back into the terminal.

"Wait!" Bill yelled. "There's so much we need to know! What about the rest of the country? How bad is the contamination? We need to know!"

Deckard didn't hear him; he was already moving deeper into the room, smoke billowing from his cigar as he walked past a few soldiers sitting at monitors. The security door slammed shut, and the soldiers surrounded the survivors, herding them into a circle. Bill reached for his .38 out of instinct and cursed—it had been the first thing the soldiers had taken when they'd captured him.

"Move along," one of the soldiers said. "Cooperate and you'll be fine."

If Bill was right, the red-headed soldier Connelly was the unit leader; the other men seemed to look to him for orders and approval. Most of the soldiers looked like they were just out of high school; only a few appeared older than twenty and only a few of them were women. It was like they were all cadets, still in boot camp and not fully prepared to fight.

But the rifles they held were still deadly. "Come on, people," Bill said to his friends. "Let's do what they tell us; it's not like we have a choice."

"Smart man," Connelly said. "Maybe you'll actually live to see another day, especially after Dr. Frankenstein gets through with you."

The other soldiers chuckled.

"Dr. Frankenstein? Who the hell's that?" Melissa asked, fear clearly showing in her eyes.

"Don't worry, lady, you'll find out. If I was you, though, I wouldn't be in a hurry to meet him."

More chuckles filled the terminal, and Marie and Bill shared a look.

Connelly ordered them to move out, waving his rifle aggressively.

Bill put his arm around Tessa, with Kenny and Phillip close by. Melissa was with Janice, who was on her feet and feeling better.

"Lead the way," Bill said politely, as if he and the others were guests instead of prisoners.

Two soldiers led the group deeper into the terminal while the other soldiers walked right behind them.

Marie moved as close as she could to Bill. "What the hell are we going to do?" she whispered. "What do they want with us?"

"I have no idea, but with the firepower they have, we're helpless to resist; we might as well play along. At least we're safe for the moment."

Marie nodded. She didn't like his answer, but it was the best they could do.

With their footsteps echoing off the terminal walls, the survivors moved deeper into the airport, not knowing where they were being led, but praying it was better from where they came.

CHAPTER 22

Bill and the others were ordered to stop when they reached the United Airlines terminal. Connelly jogged to the front of the line and continued moving forward into the terminal while the others waited nervously.

No one knew what was happening or why they'd been brought to this place, but despite the rifles aimed at them, all were curious. Connelly returned a few minutes later and waved them through a set of double doors, his face set in stone.

Bill and Marie were the first through the egress and their eyes opened wide when they took in their surroundings. A massive hangar stood before them, totally enclosed. Large air filters surrounded the massive air conditioning units that kept the hangar relatively cool.

The survivors were instructed to move to the rear of the hangar where large steel cubicles had been erected. The metal had been welded together rather shabbily, but if Bill knew the military, then the welds would withstand whatever they were designed for.

Both he and Marie were told to step inside the first cubicle and the soldiers shut them in. Bill immediately reached for the small door handle and pushed, but the door refused to budge. He could hear his friends raising their voices as they were placed in the cubicles next to his.

He sighed, realizing he was now officially a prisoner. Marie had taken a seat on the small cot in the corner of the room, the only other furniture being a small chemical toilet.

"Well, it looks like we're the official guests of the United States Army," Bill said sadly.

Marie leaned against the wall, the cool of the metal penetrating her shirt. "Well, at least we're safe for the moment. Not like anything can get us in here. Did you see those fences when we came into the airport? I couldn't be sure, but I think they were electrified."

Bill shook his head. "I fell asleep, didn't see a thing. What else did you see?" He sat next to her on the cot. It creaked beneath their weight, but seemed structurally sound.

Marie creased her forehead, trying to recall everything she'd observed when they'd entered the airport. "Well, for one thing they had guards posted at the main entrance, and there was a large gate set up. They had to open it manually for us. Once we'd made it through, there were patrols walking around, I guess to make sure the area was secure. You figure we'll be okay here?"

He shrugged. "I'm not sure of anything. I mean, why are we prisoners? We've done nothing wrong. And what was that crack about a doctor and using our blood to find a cure?" He stood up and walked the few feet to the far wall. He punched his own palm and spun around to look Marie straight in the eyes. "I don't like it, not one bit. I say if there's a chance, no matter how slim of getting out of here, we need to take it. Besides, if there's more of those killers out there—and there's no reason to assume there's not—then this airport is one giant target and I doubt even these soldiers could keep all of them at bay ... electric fences or not."

Marie sighed, stretching out on the cot. "Well, whatever happens, I'm exhausted. What do you say we grab some sleep and let the future come when it may?"

When she mentioned sleep, Bill felt a wave of exhaustion flood over him. He'd only drifted off for a short time in the transport and his weariness hit him hard now that he knew he could rest in relative safety.

Marie patted the cot. "Come here, handsome, there's room for two."

"Why, Marie, are you trying to get me into bed with you?"

She chuckled. "Don't flatter yourself. I mean, have you smelled yourself recently? Not that I'm as fresh as a daisy, mind you. No, I just want you to lie down next to me and let me pretend for just a little while that everything's fine and the world isn't falling apart."

He crossed the few feet and slid onto the cot, feeling her warm body next to him. She snuggled closer, shut her eyes, and within seconds she was asleep. Bill lay there listening to the thrum of the air conditioning units and the steady whir of her breathing. Not long after, he slipped into oblivion, into nightmares where he ran for his life as the beasts of Hell nipped at his heels.

But soon the nightmares dissolved into scenes from his past. He saw himself with his wife, Laura, honeymooning on a beach in Florida. She had looked so beautiful that first night on the sand, with the sunset casting her in a brilliant halo. He had taken her in his arms and had kissed her long and hard.

They raced each other back to their hotel room where they made love for the rest of the night, only falling asleep when he was too exhausted to continue; frankly he'd lost count after the third time.

The picture dissolved and shifted, and a moment later he found himself standing alone in a field outside of Chicago. When he turned to look at the city behind him, a large blast filled the horizon. The shockwave threw Bill to the grass, and he covered his head with his arms as the world exploded into a maelstrom of light and sound.

When he finally opened his eyes, Chicago was nothing more than a crater. He didn't know how, but he knew beyond a doubt that the destruction had been caused by a nuclear bomb.

Nothing but devastation surrounded him, and he wondered why he was still alive. Why hadn't he been vaporized from the initial blast along with the thousands of people in the city?

Bill reached up to rub his scalp and gasped when his hand came away with tufts of thinning hair. He started pulling out strand after strand until there was nothing left but a bloody mess of flaking skin.

Before he could even wonder what was happening, one of his teeth moved in his mouth. His tongue poked at it until he could finally reach in with two fingers and pluck it out.

The tooth easily came loose, the bloody root staring back at him. More and more fell out, and he spit them onto the ground until his upper jaw was nothing but a rim of raw, painful sockets.

Coughing up blood onto the dry grass, he looked down at his chest and legs. The skin was peeling away, his clothing already disintegrated, and he let out a howl of anguish that floated over the countryside. His legs grew weak and he fell to the dirt, parts of his arms dissolving into the mud of blood and soil.

As his eyeballs turned to soup and flowed out of their sockets, he realized why he was still alive when an entire city had burned in radioactive fire. So he could suffer.

He screamed one last time, his tongue falling from his mouth. His shrieks soon turned to gargles.

Death stood over him, looking down with its gaping skull.

"You can't save them!" Death screamed into his dissolving ear. *"I will have them all!"*

Bill tried to yell back, to tell Death he was wrong. He would find a way to save them—he'd promised.

As Bill tossed and turned in his cot, Marie tried to shake him awake.

"Hey, it's just a bad dream," she said into his ear, her own voice groggy from sleep.

Bill opened his eyes and seemed to stare at nothing, a sheen of sweat covering his face and arms. Then he went back to sleep, his chest rising and falling steadily. No more thrashing about.

Finally Marie closed her eyes and drifted back to sleep, comforted by the warm body next to her.

Bill slowly awoke, for a moment uncertain of where he was. He wasn't sure what had shaken him from his slumber, but it had been loud enough to wake him.

He sat up, now snapping fully awake. He didn't remember what he'd been dreaming about, but for some reason his resolve to fight and see his friends through their ordeal was stronger than ever. Then he heard it again, a soft rapping sound from the left side of his steel prison.

He carefully slid out from under Marie's embrace, and after stretching, stood up. Wiping drool from his chin, he moved closer to the wall and placed his ear against it—just as there was another bang from the other side. He pulled back, his ear ringing.

"What's up?" Marie asked, her voice groggy from sleep.

Bill pointed to the wall. "Someone's banging from the other side. Maybe it's one of the others."

"Well, don't just stand there," Marie told him, sitting up and stretching her aching limbs. "Answer them back."

Bill did as she directed and tapped on the wall with his knuckles. "Hello? Who's in there?"

"It's me, Tessa. I'm with Kenny and Phillip. Melissa and Janice are on the other side of me, but Melissa said they took Janice away a little while ago. The soldiers wouldn't say where they took her. Melissa is scared and so am I."

"How are the kids doing?" Bill asked.

"Okay, for now. They're sleeping right now. Phillip kept asking when he was going to see Roger. I didn't know what to say, so I lied again."

Bill nodded, but stopped when he realized she couldn't see him. "That's good, Tessa. We have enough to worry about right now; we don't need Phillip freaking out at the loss of his brother. Not right now."

"What do they want with us, Bill?" Tessa asked. "I thought the Army was on our side. They're not doing bad stuff to us like I heard about at the camp, at least not yet."

"I don't really know, Tessa, but just stay strong for a little while longer and you'll be fine. All of you will."

Luckily, Tessa couldn't see the concern on his face; morale had to stay high, or all was lost.

"Okay, Bill, I'll be strong ... for the kids."

"Good girl. Now go lie down and rest while you can, okay?"

She said she would and then the metal cubicle grew quiet with the exception of the hum of the air units.

Marie stood up and walked over to Bill, placing her head on his shoulder. "That was the right thing to tell her. If we're in trouble here then let them find out when they have to. Worrying about what's coming won't change it for the better."

Bill stepped away from her and grabbed her shoulders. "Well, I'm not waiting; I'm going to find out just what the hell they want with us right now. If I don't come back, you'll know we're in trouble, so take your first chance and try to escape. Hopefully you can grab the kids and any of the others if possible."

Marie smiled wanly. "Who do I look like, Rambo? I guess I'll try, but you just make sure to come back to me, to all of us." She leaned forward and kissed him lightly on the lips. Nothing sexual, just a show of affection. He squeezed her hands, then started to pound on the door, which rattled loudly. He hammered for five minutes straight until the door was finally opened.

"Dude, what the hell are you doing with all the noise?" asked a blue-eyed soldier—the same one as before they'd been placed into their cells, Bill noticed. Behind him was another soldier with dark black hair, holding his rifle at the ready in case Bill tried to escape. "What do you want?"

"I want to see Deckard, and if you don't take me to him, I'm gonna make so much damn racket I'll drive you guys crazy."

The soldier looked at Bill, seeing the conviction in his eyes. He sighed. "All right, fine, just let me check to make sure it's cool. Now give it a rest until I come back, okay?"

"Fine, but don't take too long," Bill said.

"What do you really think you'll accomplish by talking to the major?" Marie asked once the door had closed.

"I don't really know, but it's the best I could come up with on short notice." He paced back and forth until he grew tired, then plopped down on the cot. Marie leaned against the far corner, her arms crossed over her chest. Now it was a waiting game, hoping that Bill would be allowed to leave the cell.

"You know, you were having quite a dream earlier. Do you remember any of it?" Marie asked, trying to break the awkward silence while they waited.

Bill shook his head. "No, not really. Though I do get the faintest feeling it wasn't pleasant. I think my wife was there ... in my dream. She was young and healthy, before the cancer got hold of her."

Marie looked down at the floor. "I'm so sorry, Bill. I'm sure she was a good woman."

Bill smiled. "Thanks, yeah, she was."

Twenty minutes ticked by. Bill was starting to worry that his request had been ignored when the door to the cell swung open. The same blue-eyed soldier stood in the doorframe and he waved Bill to come out. Marie tried to follow him, but she was told to stay.

"Just him. The major's not much on the fairer sex, ma'am. He believes they're only on this earth for one thing, pardon my English."

Marie frowned. "Male chauvinist pig. I thought they were almost extinct." She trudged back to the cot and sat down.

Bill said, "Don't worry, Marie. I'll be back, I promise."

"You'd better," she said as the door closed.

"If you're going to be guarding me," Bill said to the blue-eyed soldier, "do you mind if I ask you your name?"

The man shrugged. "Sure, no biggy. The name's Private Chris Robinson and this here's Huff." He pointed to the other soldier with the black hair.

"Just Huff?" Bill asked.

Huff nodded. "That's right. Never needed anything more."

"Fair enough, Huff. I'm Bill. So, shall we go?"

They headed off, and two more soldiers replaced the men escorting him. The soldiers nodded to one another, and Chris slapped his replacement on the shoulder in greeting.

The two soldiers escorted Bill back through the terminal to the security base. Inside, the major was still in the same place, and Bill wondered if the man had ever left.

The sergeant-major turned and waved Bill forward.

Stepping onto the platform, Bill got a closer look at the monitor screens. He could see the airport's perimeter fence and front gate, as well as the main road in. Other cameras covered different parts of the terminal. Bill's eyes stopped when he saw what looked like a lab table with a corpse on top of it. The major quickly flicked a switch, changing to one of the cameras aimed at the perimeter fence.

Sergeant Major Thaddeus Deckard turned and gave Bill his full attention. "One of my men said you were being quite unruly. It was either let you see me or have you shot. Aren't you glad I chose the latter?"

Bill swallowed hard; he hadn't realized his fate had been so carelessly decided. "Yes, I am, thank you."

"So now that you're here, would you mind telling me just what the hell you want?"

Bill cleared his throat. "Well for starters, how come only a sergeant-major is running this temporary camp? Why isn't there someone of higher authority, like a colonel or a captain?"

If Deckard was offended by the inquiry, he never let on; instead he lit the cigar in his mouth and leaned back against a bank of monitors.

"There was a general in charge, but he died when our last camp was overrun by infected civilians. More than half of my men either died or became infected when their gas masks were ripped off. We don't know much about this virus, but we do know it's airborne, so to walk around outside exposed is a death warrant; that is, with the exception of a small percentage of the population that appears to be immune.

"I took command when things at the last camp fell apart. I rallied the men and grabbed what we could and bugged out, taking as many eggheads as I could find. Now those same scientists are our only hope. Driving into the airport, I figured we could do a lot worse. After all, it already has fences and security cameras, and it was already deserted once the FAA grounded all flights in or out of the United States. You see, once we were infiltrated by the infected, there was no way to leave Illinois. The entire state has been quarantined. But by now it's probably everywhere across the damn planet. Barricades have been set up around the state, and anyone trying to leave is shot on sight, infected or not, though I wonder how many of the roadblocks are still being manned by personnel. Communication has been spotty at best. So you see, if we don't find a cure here and now, we're all dead."

"So what does that have to do with me and my friends being treated like prisoners?" Bill asked.

"Well, you seem to be part of the small minority that is immune to the virus. You need to be examined, blood work and the like. Hopefully, there's something in your blood or immune system that will help the docs procure a cure."

"Okay, that's fine with me. I'm sure my friends will agree with me that we'll gladly help anyway we can. So then why are you keeping us locked up?"

Deckard shifted his feet, looking like a scolded child. "Ah, well you see, some of the procedures the doctors have to do are quite invasive. It's possible some of you might die. At least that's what's happened to the few other immune people we've come across. But don't worry; your deaths will be for the greater good. In fact, you might be the one to save humanity." He grinned at the end of his speech, proud of what he was doing.

"What? Are you mad? Killing me or my friends won't find you a cure, no matter how much you dig into us. If it's not in a simple blood sample then it's not there to find!"

Deckard waved to the two soldiers at the door to come and hold Bill.

Bill struggled for a moment, but soon realized he was easily overpowered, so he decided to bide his time and pray for an opportunity to escape.

Deckard leaned forward and blew smoke into Bill's face. "I'm sorry it has to be this way, I really am, but there's no other choice. I'm sure you've heard the saying, 'the good of the many is more important than the good of the one.' This is one of those cases." Deckard turned to Private Chris Robinson while smoke rings surrounded his head like a sick parody of a halo.

"Private Robinson, take this man to the doc now instead of later. Have him sedated and tell the doc to make him his next test subject."

"Yes, Sergeant Major," Chris said as he started to drag Bill out of the security base.

"Oh, and Private, tell the doc it would be nice if he left this one alive, but to do what he has to do. Results are the important thing."

"Yes, Sergeant Major, I'll tell him." Chris exited the room, with Huff on the other side.

Bill wanted to push both soldiers away from him and run for it, but there was nowhere to go. And if he did manage to elude his pursuers, he couldn't escape and leave his friends to a horrible fate at the hands of a mad doctor.

Shrugging the two men off him, he straightened his back and looked Chris in the eyes.

"Well, come on then, let's get to it, I don't have all day." Almost dragging the two soldiers behind him, Bill moved off into the terminal, Chris telling him if he was going the right way.

While he walked between the two guards, Bill wracked his brain for a way out. To have survived so much only to be used as a lab experiment by his elected government was inexcusable. He had to find a way out. A distraction maybe, but what kind of distraction could be so big that he would have free reign of the terminal and still be able to rescue his friends?

With all these questions floating around inside his head, he moved closer and closer to a meeting with the revered Dr. Frankenstein.

He knew he wasn't going to like what was going to happen next, but he was powerless to stop it ... at least for the moment.

CHAPTER 23

While the walk to the lab was uneventful, Bill took full use of the time to get the lay of the land. His eyes constantly scanned every door and access vent that led into the ceiling. He didn't know what he would do with the information, but he felt every bit of info might come in handy.

As they walked down the center of the terminal, Bill noticed the lack of personnel. When he had first arrived he'd had the feeling there was a full complement of soldiers, but the more he watched, he realized he was seeing the same people more than once while they moved about the terminal on various errands.

"Where is everybody?" Bill asked casually. "Why aren't there more soldiers around here?"

Private Chris Robinson shrugged. "We lost almost everybody when we evacuated the camp. I witnessed our first commander dragged off by a large group of infected. His screams were so loud I could hear them over everyone else's." He seemed to hesitate for a moment and then he pushed on. "Then he stopped screaming and I didn't hear him after that."

Bill waited to hear more, but that was all the soldier was going to give him. Bill watched the young man's face while they walked. Whatever he'd seen had shaken him up pretty bad.

"I'm sorry about your commander and everyone else that was killed, but I don't see why me and my friends have to die on the off chance some quack might find a cure."

Chris slowed as he looked to Bill. "Oh no, sir. Dr. Stevens is one of the leading epidemiologists in his field. If anyone can find a cure, it's him. It's just he's a little too aggressive with his research. I'm sorry about that, but the sergeant major says it's for the better good. If a few people die and we save millions, billions even ... well, isn't that an okay price to pay?"

Bill stopped walking, the other soldier aggravated by the holdup. "Listen, son, I'm older than you and I hope you'll think about what I'm going to tell you. If I thought for just one second that if I gave my life there could be a cure, I would. But I won't just throw it away while some nut plays doctor on the off chance he might get lucky. Do you understand what I'm trying to say?"

Chris nodded and turned away from Bill's deep gaze.

"Yeah, I do, but it's out of my hands. My orders are to bring you to the doc and that's what I'm gonna do. Now if it's all the same to you, talk time's over."

Bill was about to say something else, but the look in Chris' eyes said he meant what he said. Huff shoved Bill forward with the butt of his rifle and Bill started forward again.

No one talked the rest of the way to the lab.

When Bill reached the research lab, he saw it was the tent-like structure he had originally passed when first entering the terminal with the others. Everything was a bright white and the smell of bleach filled the room. Two soldiers stood at the opening; both seemed bored at standing guard duty.

Inside the tent, the two soldiers strapped Bill to a metal table, then with an almost rueful look from Chris, they left. Bill stared at the ceiling, his blood pounding in his chest. The actual ceiling was hidden by the tent's roof, the material sagging in places and billowing in others as the vents blew in fresh air.

Bill turned his head at the sound of footsteps behind him. Though the person was coming closer, he still couldn't turn his head far enough to see who it was. He could only assume it was the fabled Dr. Stevens, or as the soldiers called him, Dr. Frankenstein.

Bill noticed another table a few feet to his left. A sheet covered what had to be a body, the material stained red, the deep vermillion color a sharp contrast to the rest of the room.

Bill looked up as a shadow fell across him and he came face to face with Dr. Stevens for the first time. The man was unassuming. He had a thinning hairline with a heavy brow, thin cheeks and an almost nonexistent chin. His pale complexion suggested that he didn't get out much and that natural sunlight was alien to his skin.

Dr. Stevens looked down on Bill and grinned. The smile showed neither malice nor kindness. It simply was. As if the man had learned to mimic the simple social graces from a book but had yet to practice them on a real person.

"Good afternoon, sir. I'm Dr. Stevens," he said in a high-pitched, nasally voice. "Thank you for volunteering to help find a cure to this epidemic. If it weren't for people like you, I fear there might never be a cure."

Bill's mouth fell open. "Volunteer? Are you crazy? I was forced to come here! I don't want to help you—now let me out of here, or so help me ..."

Dr. Stevens held up a hand as if silencing a young child short on manners. "Uh-uh, well, whether you volunteered or not really isn't the question. The question is, why do you seem to be immune to the disease while thousands, if not millions, have already succumbed to it?" He reached around his back and pulled a table full of surgical implements closer to him. "Now,

I'm afraid some of the tests I'll be doing are quite invasive, painful actually, but that can't be helped." He scanned the tray for something he couldn't seem to find, then sighed and stepped away from Bill. "Well, it seems I don't have all the scalpels I need. Some of them are probably still being sterilized from the last specimen. I'll be right back, so you just try to stay calm and don't go anywhere." He chuckled at his poor joke and patted Bill's shoulder, almost tenderly. "Don't worry, the pain will be quick. I promise." He slipped away into the back of the room, out of sight. He mumbled about the lack of manpower and how he had to do almost everything himself.

When he walked by the nearby surgical table, his waist rubbed and shifted the sheet covering the bloody lump. The doctor never noticed.

Bill's face went white and a scream locked in his chest. Across from him, no more than three feet away, was the desecrated body of Janice. Her chest was peeled open in a macabre illusion of an autopsy, only her face was frozen in a mask of pain and terror. Whatever Dr. Stevens had done to her, she had suffered terribly. She must have been the last specimen he had referred to.

Janice's eyes were still open, gazing up at the white tent ceiling. Her dead stare unnerved Bill the most, and he became almost hypnotized by them.

He realized he would be next, and if it wasn't him, then Tessa or Marie would find themselves strapped to Dr. Stevens' table of horrors.

Though he felt terrible for her death, deep down inside himself, where no one else would ever go, he breathed a sigh of relief. It could have been him on that table.

He struggled with the straps securing his arms and legs.

At first nothing happened, but then he realized the strap on his right arm, the one Chris had secured, was more slack than the others. The private had buckled the strap one notch looser. Bill pulled as hard as he could, knowing there was only seconds before the mad doctor returned.

The sharp leather cut into his flesh, yet he pulled harder, biting back a yelp of pain and grimacing as he started to see black spots in front of his eyes.

The blood worked as a lubricant; his hand slipped free, but his thumb cracked the wrong way.

Breathing in great gasps, Bill looked down at his hand and was shocked to see the skin between his wrist and hand almost completely peeled away, hanging in ribbons. Blood covered the area, keeping the air from stinging the wound too badly, and though the limb felt like it was on fire, he quickly but clumsily undid the other strap and then released his feet.

He heard rattling behind him, and he reached out, grabbed one of the half dozen scalpels on the nearby cart and lay back down. He could only hope the doctor didn't notice his bleeding wrist until he was closer.

So far the two soldiers on guard duty were still oblivious, chatting idly, uninterested in the goings-on in the lab.

Dr. Stevens walked back to Bill's side, a tray of instruments in his hands.

"Ah, here we go, all nice and clean and ready for business. I'm sorry if I've kept you waiting, but it's just that—"

Bill sat up and swiped the scalpel across the man's throat, severing the carotid artery in one clean motion; blood shot out and gurgled up and bathed Bill in viscous warmth. The razor-sharp knife almost felt like it was passing through air. Bill had been prepared for some resistance when the blade touched flesh, but there had been almost no resistance at all.

Dr. Stevens dropped, his instruments falling to the floor with a metallic clatter.

The two soldiers turned to see what was happening in the lab. What they expected to see was Dr. Stevens picking something up, not a man with a scalpel in each hand, charging them like a maniac covered in blood.

The soldiers tried to take aim, but Bill shoved them into the fabric of the tent, ripping through it.

He stabbed both soldiers in the chest at almost the exact same time, slicing the first private's heart nearly in two, killing him before his body struck the floor. The second soldier was more fortunate: the blade missed his heart and anything vital, slipping through his ribcage and piercing muscle and veins.

If the soldier had been able to leave the scalpel in so he could seek medical attention, his odds of living would have been excellent, but the man squirmed away and the blade came free as he retreated. Bill managed to twist the instrument, doubling the wound in size.

Blood shot outward and the man's chest was soaked in seconds.

The soldier tried to crawl away, reaching for his sidearm. Bill cut himself free of the tent. He fell onto the soldier and slashed and slashed until all he saw was red.

Only seconds had passed, but Bill was lost in limbo as he vented his fury on the unfortunate soldier. When he was finished, he looked down at the bloody mess that was once a human being and immediately felt sick. He had lost total control and had taken out all his anger and frustration on the poor man.

Standing up, he tried to wipe some of the blood from his face, but the effort was futile.

The terminal was empty. He knew it wouldn't last, though. Any second someone would come around the corner, see the mess and sound the alarm. Bill needed to move—fast.

The other soldier's blood had sprayed his lime t-shirt, but the green jacket and pants of his uniform were mostly untouched, except for the occasional heavy drops of blood here and there.

Wasting no time, Bill stripped the soldier of his jacket, pants and hat, then grabbed the rifle and sidearm and ran off down the corridor for a place to hide.

He saw signs for the bathrooms. With the lack of women in the terminal, he decided he would be less likely to be discovered in the ladies' room, so he slipped inside.

He leaned against the door and tried to slow his breathing, tried to stop shaking. He'd killed three people in as many minutes and the shock was already hitting him, despite the fact that it was either him or them.

Bill washed his face in the sink and pulled his shirt off. His wrist was stinging something awful now that his adrenaline was seeping away. He stared at his reflection in the mirror, stared deep into his own eyes. Is this what he had become now? A killer who would take a life without a moment of thought?

Pushing the troubling thoughts away, he focused on the immediate problems: his wound, his escape.

He quickly changed out of his pants and shirt and into the soldier's clothes. The pants were too tight, the jacket too short around the arms, but it would fool anyone giving him a cursory look. The hat worked well to cover his face, but it was far too big for his head and hung loosely over his eyes. Uncomfortable, but still useful.

After rinsing his bloody shirt in the sink, he ripped it to rags and wrapped some of them around his wrist wound. He held back a scream and closed his eyes to control his dimming vision.

He leaned against the long vanity counter and concentrated on breathing, relieved when his arm subsided to a dull throb.

When he was sure he wouldn't faint and he thought the shaking was under control, he slipped out of the bathroom.

Soldiers were already on the scene, investigating the attack. Bill quietly disappeared around the next junction to the terminal.

One or two personnel saw him, but no one was looking for an intruder wearing the same uniform as them, so Bill made it away free and clear.

Not sure where he was going, but just wanting to hide and figure out a way to save his friends, he ran deeper into the airport.

CHAPTER 24

Marie paced back and forth in her small metal cell. Bill had been gone for more than an hour and she could only pray he was all right. Tessa kept her company, the two women talking through the thin metal. Tessa relayed words of encouragement to Melissa, who was also alone in her cell. Melissa kept asking about Janice, but none of them knew anything new.

"How are the kids doing?" Marie asked Tessa.

"They're okay. They're playing in the corner. Kenny found a piece of paper under our cot and he made a paper plane out of it. Phillip loves it."

"That's good. The longer they stay busy, the less we have to tell them," Marie said. She could only hope it never came to the point that the children found out what their fates might be.

Sitting down on the cot, she stared up at the ceiling high above her. Though the metal crossbeams would be easy to walk on, there was no way to reach them. The walls of the cell were smooth, and they stopped long before reaching the first and lowest rafter. The only way out of her cell was through the door.

"What do you think is happening to Bill?" Tessa asked through the wall. "Do you think he's all right?"

Marie let out a sigh. "Honestly, honey, I just don't know. These soldiers don't seem to care much for us or they wouldn't have locked us up like some kind of criminals."

"But we're safe here, right? I mean, none of those crazy people can get us in here. You saw the fences when we entered this morning."

"Yes, honey, we're safe here," Marie lied. "We shouldn't have to worry anymore. Once the government gets a handle on things, everything will be back to normal before you know it."

"That's good. I'm gonna lie down for a while, but just tap on the wall if you want to talk."

"Okay, honey, have a good rest." Under her breath Marie added, "You'll need it."

Stretching her legs out in front of her, Marie let out a sigh and tried to relax. Whatever happened next was out of her hands, but she had an overwhelming feeling of dread she just couldn't shake.

When she was a little girl, she'd had nightmares for almost two weeks about her pet cat, Pickles. Her parents had told her they were just dreams, but two weeks to the day, Pickles was run over by a car. Though she had been an inside cat, she had somehow managed to get out for the first time ever and had been run down in the street. Marie's father had found the cat dead in the gutter, its intestines trailing behind it. She had run out to say goodbye to her father as he left for work and found him carrying her beloved pet on a shovel. She had cried for a week after that.

Years later, she'd had continuous nightmares of her mother dying only days before receiving a phone call that her mother had indeed died from a heart attack in the middle of the night.

Though she was in no way psychic, she had always been sensitive to bad things happening. She had learned to trust her instincts and had never told another soul about them. And now, as she leaned her head against the cool metal of her prison wall, she felt that same feeling again.

Whatever was coming, she knew it was going to be big.

Dean slowed at the head of his massive army to rest a while. One of his scouts had reported activity at Midway airport.

"So they went to the airport, eh? Makes sense. It's secure with a large fence surrounding it. Since 9/11, airports are like small forts in themselves."

Standing next to Dean, relishing the time to rest, Mike raised a question. "So you're really going to kill everyone you find? How could any of the normal people like me threaten you?"

"How? By existing, that's how. Normals and Changed are different animals now. One is the hunter and the other is the prey. Guess which one you are?" Dean clucked happily.

Mike didn't answer, looking back on the wave of heads behind them. The hardest part of the forced march from Chicago had been finding food and water to keep the people healthy. Luckily, a supermarket had been on their route, and Dean had sent the Changed into the store to salvage what they could find. What they found was a family of normals hiding in the back. The family was quickly slaughtered and thrown out near the store's dumpster.

The Changed had consumed everything in the supermarket, leaving only a few crumbs and a mountain of trash, ripping open packages of meat and devouring the food whole. The power was still on, some electric plant running on automatic for the time being, so the meat had been kept fresh.

Mike had watched the infected pour out of the doors with their prizes in hand, and he wondered how many would get sick from eating the raw meat. Or worse, how many would get a serious case of the runs?

Dean had handed him a box of pretzels, and Mike had shoved them into his mouth in handfuls. With nothing to drink, his mouth had felt like a desert, but they soon came upon a small stream where almost all of the massive army slaked their thirst.

Deciding he'd rested long enough, Dean started walking again, his army following him like lovesick puppies. Their howls for blood and screams of rage had driven Mike crazy at first, but now he barely heard them.

For the moment, Dean was quiet and Mike knew better than to break the man's ruminations. Sometimes Dean would talk for hours, sharing things that had happened to him and what the change had done to him. Mike listened to everything he said, afraid of what would happen if he appeared uninterested.

He wasn't an optimist, but he still had hope he would somehow live through this ordeal. He wondered if this was his punishment for leaving Becky to die. He doubted it, but the irony was still with him.

A stray dog ran across the highway ahead, and more than a hundred of the Changed dashed after it, howling and screaming for its blood. Dean threw his hands into the air in frustration.

This wasn't the first time this had happened. A few miles back, a squirrel had darted from the shoulder of the road, and more than two hundred had chased it into the scrub brush, blind to the bank on the other side—they all tumbled helplessly down the hill. More than fifty died, crushed by their fellow brethren; others just shattered or broke their limbs.

Dean had left them to rot in the sun, too disgusted to deal with the situation. Though the Changed followed him loyally, they weren't very bright. Only with a firm hand had Dean managed to gather so many in one place, and he sometimes wondered if he could maintain his control over them.

That's why it was important to reach the airport as soon as possible. Only when the Changed had prey to attack were they fully under his control.

Deciding the ones that had chased after the dog were irrelevant to his grand design, Dean waved the others onward, leading the way like a medieval knight going to war.

CHAPTER 25

Bill was running and hiding as he made his way through the airport terminal. Whenever he heard footsteps, he immediately darted into an alcove and waited while the approaching soldiers marched by. Less than ten minutes had passed since he'd left the bathroom, and so far the personnel had barely noticed him, his stolen uniform the perfect disguise.

He slowly made his way back toward the hangar. While he didn't know for sure whether his friends were still there, he had nowhere else to go. So foot by agonizing foot, he kept moving, expecting to be discovered every time he turned a corner.

He almost fired the rifle when an alarm started to sound, filling the terminal with its loud shriek. The soldiers must have found the two men he had killed. Now the whole airport was on red alert.

Bill rounded a corner at an intersection—and walked straight into two soldiers running full tilt the opposite way. All three of them fell to the floor in a heap of flailing limbs and weapons.

Bill reached for his rifle and pulled it to him just as the other two men sat up.

"You moron," the first soldier said, a man in his late forties with thinning hair and a large wart on his chin. "Why don't you watch where you're going? The sergeant-major said the disturbance is happening behind you. Why are you going the wrong way?"

Bill's mouth hung open. He was caught flatfooted.

"Yeah, pal, you need to follow us," the other soldier said, a short man in his late twenties with a pointed noise and thin lips. He had bags under his eyes. From lack of sleep. "Hey, what happened to your arm?"

"Um, sorry," Bill said as the two soldiers climbed to their feet and slung their rifles casually over their shoulders. "I guess I got turned around." He didn't sound very convincing, even to himself.

At that precise moment Soldier Number One's radio squawked. "Attention, all personnel: the attacker is wearing one of our uniforms. Be on the lookout for anyone who looks suspicious. Due to the amount of blood on the scene, he is probably wounded, over." Soldier Number Two looked down at Bill's wounded wrist and his eyes went wide. "Holy shit, this guy's—"

Bill fired his weapon from the hip, angling it upward; the bullet struck the soldier in the neck and passed straight through the back of his head to lodge in the acoustic ceiling tiles above.

The soldier instinctually reached up to the pain and was shocked to see his hand come away bathed in red. His mouth continued to open and close, and his knees gave out from under him. He fell to the polished floor of the terminal, gargling up a few more splats of blood.

The other man snarled and cursed and tried to sling his rifle over his shoulder to take aim, but Bill, using his own barrel as a makeshift sword, blocked the man's gun and kneed him in the balls.

The breath whooshed from the soldier's lungs as he doubled over, and he let out a dry wheeze while he tried to suck in air. Bill never gave him the chance. He lifted the rifle stock over his head and brought it down with bone-crushing force on the back of the man's neck.

The hard plastic stock vibrated with the impact, and Bill winced as his arms absorbed the brunt of it. The soldier dropped to the floor. His fingers twitched. Blood dripped from his mouth.

Bill sighed. Counting these two men, he had killed five people in almost the same amount of time, give or take a few minutes. If things kept up like this, he would be adding a lot more to his list, as long as they didn't get him first.

More footsteps echoed down the wide terminal. Quickly, ignoring the throbbing in his wrist, Bill retrieved the combat blade from the first soldier's hip; it could prove useful as a stealth weapon.

He ran to a side door and started down a small utility tunnel parallel with the main terminal, keeping his rifle in front of him, prepared to fire at the first sign of movement, hoping he was still moving the right way in his search for Marie and the others.

His footsteps grew louder as he moved deeper into the utility tunnel. Some of the overhead lights had gone out; evidently the maintenance staff hadn't been on top of their game.

He slowed to a walk, periodically hearing shouts and boot steps coming from the other side of the wall on his left.

With the death of the last two soldiers, he was pretty sure the rest of the airport personnel would be out to get him. He wiped some of the blood from his face, spray from the soldier he'd shot through the neck.

He sighed deeply, trying to get his breathing under control. How had it come to this? A week ago life had been normal.

True, he hadn't been the happiest man alive. Not after his wife's death.

Thinking of Laura made him smile wanly. He remembered the smell of her hair, the way little wrinkles appeared next to her eyes when she smiled. And she had smiled a lot. Bill had always done his best to make her happy. Theirs had been a whirlwind relationship. They had met on the "L" train one day, pushed so close together by the crowd that he could smell her perfume. Though they hadn't talked, their eyes had constantly met.

When the train had reached the next stop, she had poured out of the car along with twenty other passengers, and Bill had watched her go sadly. He had chastised himself for not saying something to her, but what do you say to a woman you've just met on a train?

For two days, he'd searched for her while he rode the train to and from work, but she was nowhere to be found. She was gone.

On the third day, he had given up hope until he'd looked up from his newspaper to see her standing at the rear of the car. Just as he spotted her, the train lurched to a stop and she stepped out onto the platform. Throwing caution to the wind, he ran after her, despite being three stops from his destination. They both reached street level at the same moment, and with the John Hancock Center looming over them, he caught up to her. Though he knew he was crazy, he stopped her and introduced himself. At first she wasn't interested, but Bill continued to charm her and make her laugh and she finally agreed to coffee later in the day.

Bill left for work, late thanks to his detour. The rest of the day went agonizingly slow; the only thing on his mind was Laura. He hadn't gotten her phone number, and if she changed her mind or had just outright lied, he'd never find her again.

At five o'clock, Bill was the first one out the door. His heart beat so fast as he rode the train to the Hancock Center he thought the other people in the car would stare at him, wondering what was wrong with him. But no one did, and he reached his destination.

He took the stairs three at a time and wormed his way through the throng of pedestrians on the street, and when the last person blocking his view moved out of the way, he slowed and looked into the coffee shop. There, inside, on the other side of the large pane of glass that made up the front of the building, sat Laura.

She had come. He quickly moved inside and sat down, talking and making her laugh once more. Six months later they married and lived happily together for the next twenty years. The rest was history.

The sound of scraping pulled Bill from his reverie. The tunnel curved to the right, so he wasn't able to see what was making the noise.

Soldiers, maybe, dozens of them preparing to come around the corner, guns blasting. Or maybe some of the infected, hands out and teeth gnashing, ready to tear the flesh from his bones.

He swallowed hard and pushed the thoughts from his mind. Getting worked up now would do nothing but get him killed.

Holding the rifle ready to fire, Bill crept forward. The scraping sound slowly moved toward him. He stopped when he thought he heard the sound behind him as well, but assumed it must be the service tunnel's acoustics playing tricks on him.

Reaching the slight curve, he poked his head around. His breath caught in his throat.

A large German shepherd was slowly creeping forward, its claws scraping on the cement floor. The harness it had worn as a Customs dog still hung from its neck and shoulders. The animal's muzzle flared and its teeth shined with a slight tint of red.

It growled at him.

Bill took two steps backward, bringing the rifle up, ready to put a round through the dog's head—until he heard shouting and footsteps on the other side of the wall.

Soldiers were patrolling the terminal, looking for him, and if he shot the dog, they would immediately know where he was.

Another growl came from his rear, yet another Customs dog behind him. This one looked worse, its ribs showing under the disheveled fur.

These dogs had probably been trapped in the service tunnels for almost a week. They were hungry, and Bill's ass was the blue plate special.

The first dog moved closer, its hackles raised, its haunches high as it prepared to attack; the other moved low to the floor, evidently waiting for his brother to do the dirty work.

Holding the rifle like a club, Bill swallowed hard and waited, smiling at the dogs as they moved closer. They could smell the blood on his cut wrist and clothing.

"Easy, boy, there's a good boy. Now why don't we just be friends?"

The dog would have none of it. Its rear legs tensed, and Bill knew what was coming next. He couldn't run, blocked by the second animal, and he found it somewhat amusing how after everything he'd been through, he was about to be taken down by a couple of domesticated, yet hungry, dogs.

And then it happened.

The first one jumped at Bill, its teeth flashing.

He swung the rifle as hard as he could, slashing his hand on the gun sight at the end of the barrel, swatting the dog away from his throat. But the animal still struck his right shoulder, and he fell to the floor as the dog rolled over him. The rifle slid across the concrete and stopped against a pile of wires against the far wall.

One of the dog's back claws had scraped his left thigh, and he let out a short yell that he quickly stifled. It was bad enough he had to defend himself against two animals in the small confines of the tunnel, but he had to do it without firing a shot or making a sound.

The second dog pounced, going for Bill's throat. He reached out with his free hand and grabbed a stray pipe lying in the tunnel. He thrust it into the dog's mouth, fending off the savage attack, while the other animal circled him, looking for an opening.

Not wanting to get to close, it tried to nip at his shoes, but the hard leather prevented any serious damage to his feet.

Bill struggled with the animal, its fetid breath enough to gag him. The German shepherd was light, having lost most of its body mass from lack of nourishment; Bill rolled to the side and threw it against the wall. It yelped and rolled back to its feet. Bill used the precious second to pull the combat knife from its sheath clipped to his pants.

The first dog had jumped into the fray, only hesitating for an instant when it was sure its partner was still mobile.

Bill had a fleeting thought. If he could disable or even kill one of them, perhaps the other would leave him be and finish off the wounded animal. It was a chance he would have to take; there was no way he could kill both dogs without being seriously injured.

Both dogs let out low growls, and Bill waved the blade in front of him. With each slash of the knife, the dogs retreated. Evidently, they knew what it was and respected it. Bill tried to back away from the German shepherds, but the skinnier one slipped behind him, blocking his retreat.

Cursing the dog's intelligence, Bill made a tough decision, realizing he was going to lose.

Baring his own teeth, he crouched, flexed his legs, and jumped onto the first dog, barely avoiding the snapping muzzle as he plunged the blade to the hilt into the animal's side. The dog screeched and tried to escape.

Bill pulled the blade free, grasping the dog's control harness for leverage, and then he slammed the knife into its body once again. The dog seemed to shake and then slow its snapping as blood shot out of the first wound, painting the wall a bright crimson. Blood frothed around its muzzle, and its breathing grew labored.

The second dog hesitated, mostly a follower, subservient to the wounded dog. Bill used the animal's cowardice and snarled at it, the wet blade spattering its nose and eyes with small droplets of vermilion.

The dog's head went low to the ground, the smell of blood driving it wild despite its fear.

Bill crawled backwards on his hands and knees, the knife always in front of him.

The wounded animal stood up, unsteady on its feet, the loss of blood already slowing it down. The second dog moved closer, sniffing the air. It turned once to glare at Bill, its eyes flaring in the dim light, then it turned to watch its brother.

The wounded dog slumped to the floor, its eyes thin slits, each breath more and more labored. Bloody bubbles pushed from one of the wounds, telling Bill he'd struck a lung.

He crawled away from the two animals, cursing his luck that the rifle was on the other side of them.

When he was almost fifteen feet away, he saw what he expected. The second animal bit into the other's neck and shook its head back and forth, shredding muscle and tendon. The wounded dog let out one muffled yelp and then fell silent. Next came the sound of ripping and chewing.

Bill rolled to his knees and backed away as fast as possible. A few times he backed into the wall, but he refused to take his eyes off the feral animals.

When he was far enough away that he felt secure, he picked a door at random and exited the service tunnel. He had no idea if there were more roaming in between the walls of the airport, but he couldn't risk another encounter with wild animals.

The terminal was empty, and a fine layer of dust coated the floor; he could tell no one had used this part of the airport for at least a few days.

Made sense. The soldiers needed to keep their part of the terminal airtight or risk the airborne virus infecting them.

As he ran onward, feeling vulnerable, Bill thought about the virus and the air containment. Maybe he could use that as a weapon to free his friends. But if he let the virus inside the protected airport terminal, he would still have to deal with the soldiers, only then they would be infected and even hungrier for his blood. At least now they were under orders from their commander, still governed by some semblance of humanity.

Private Chris Robinson was proof of that.

With all these ideas floating through his mind, and with his wrist throbbing from his tussle with the dogs, he ran deeper into the new terminal, deciding he needed to find another bathroom so he could wash up and rest.

CHAPTER 26

"Report! What the hell is going on out there?" Sergeant-Major Thaddeus Deckard screamed at the two subordinates standing in front of him.

"Um, well, Sergeant-Major, we're still trying to piece together what happened, but it appears one of Dr. Stevens' patients got loose and killed him and then took out both of the guards." The man said this all with a sheepish look, afraid to make eye contact with the furious sergeant-major.

"What? How? I want this place locked down now! Find out who did this and bring me their heads."

Both men saluted and turned to leave. Before the last soldier walked out the door, Deckard said, "Private, one more thing. When you bring me that head, I don't really give a damn if it's still attached to the body."

The man saluted and turned to leave. "Understood, Sergeant-Major."

Deckard turned to the two specialists monitoring the security system monitors. "We have all these damn cameras and no one saw anything? Why the hell not?"

Mr. Batton, a young soldier with acne still covering his cheeks, looked up at Deckard. "It's not our fault, sir, I swear. There aren't any cameras where the temporary clinic was set up, and Dr. Stevens said he didn't want any. He said they were an invasion of his privacy."

"Privacy? He's in the Army, for Christ's sake! If we had a security camera in there, none of this would've happened."

He turned when another soldier entered the room, holding a piece of paper, which he meekly handed to Deckard before vacating. Deckard read the letter quickly, his teeth showing as veins popped on his forehead.

"Jesus damn Christ, that son of a bitch has killed two more of my men. So help me, when I get hold of him, he'll pray we killed him on the spot." Turning to the second man at the monitors, Mr. Smith, he leaned forward, the unlit cigar moving up and down while he talked. "Sound the alarm. I want every available man and woman looking for that bastard. Shoot on sight, but try to bring him in alive."

"Yes, sir, I'll get right on it."

Deckard frowned and glanced at Mr. Batton. "Fine. And the both of you listen up. Stop calling me sir. I'm not a damn officer, I work for a living!"

"Yes ... yes, Sergeant-Major," Mr. Batton said, Smith nodding in agreement.

"Good, carry on then."

Deckard moved to the large office chair in the center of the room and sat down. He stretched his legs and bit off a soggy piece of cigar. Though he had found plenty in one of the gift shops scattered across the terminal, he enjoyed making them last. It reminded him of his days on the battlefield when he never knew where his next cigar would come from, so he had to make the one he had last as long as possible.

For almost forty-two years Deckard had been in the United States Army. He had joined right out of high school and had fought in almost every war since. When he wore his dress uniform, his chest looked like a rainbow salad with all the metals he'd won or received.

No one would ever accuse Thaddeus Deckard of being a coward. He wished he could grab his silver-plated Desert Eagle and join his men in the hunt for the escaped prisoner, but someone needed to coordinate the operation. No, his days of fighting were mostly over. Now he would lead and let the young do the dirty work, though it burned him to do so.

Chewing contently on the end of his cigar, Deckard watched the monitors where his men and a few women moved about the terminal. They would find the fugitive, he had no doubt. The airport was like an island surrounded by fire. Chicago was ash, along with the suburbs, the conflagration still spreading. If rain didn't come soon, the whole damn state could go up in a giant fireball. Where would the fugitive go?

Deckard leaned forward in his chair, the leather creaking beneath him.

"Mr. Batton, has there been any word from Washington or any of the other rescue camps?"

Batton shook his head. "Negative, sir ... I mean, Sergeant-Major. The lines have been down for almost two days now."

"What about the two-way? Any chatter there?"

"Negative there as well. All we've picked up is static. If there was someone monitoring our bandwidth, I believe they would have answered by now." Batton sat up a little straighter; he looked worried. "Can I speak freely, Sergeant-Major?"

Deckard nodded curtly. "Of course, I always value the opinion of my men; only a damn fool thinks he knows it all."

Mr. Batton seemed to wiggle in his seat as if sitting on something uncomfortable. "Well, me and the other guys have been talking and we all agree that we might be the only camp left in the entire Chicago area, and if so, what do you want to do about it? Should we stay here or try to make a run for stable ground?"

Deckard had been thinking the same thing, but hadn't wanted to alarm any of his men. Without hope, men fighting a war were lost before they began the battle.

"I think for the time being we should concentrate on apprehending the escaped prisoner and finding a cure for this damn virus before we all become stark raving lunatics. Now back to your station, if you please."

Mr. Batton nodded and turned back to his monitors.

Another private handed Deckard a report about what was being done to find the prisoner. She was a pretty young thing in her early thirties, but to Deckard, only competence mattered, and she was a good soldier. He dismissed her and scanned the report. He tried not to think too much about how almost all the personnel below him now were privates. There were a few sergeants and one or two majors, but no one had any field experience, so Deckard had taken the mantle of command. He had never risen high in the Army, satisfied to stay with his men. He always felt when you became a colonel or general, all the statistics and collateral damages numbed and blinded you to what really mattered: those men and women behind the faceless numbers.

So he had stayed a sergeant-major, despite the numerous chances to rise further in the ranks. He never regretted it for a minute.

Leaning back in his oversized chair, he decided it was time to light his cigar. Puffing hard, he lit the tip, the wet end filling his mouth with the flavor of tobacco. He let out a sigh and closed his eyes for a moment, trying to visualize himself on a beach in Hawaii, the relaxing sound of the surf, a gentle breeze on his scarred face. And for the hell of it, a few island girls rubbing his shoulders and feet.

"Sergeant-Major, I think we've found him," Mr. Batton said excitedly.

Deckard jumped from the chair and looked over the man's shoulder. "Where is he? Report damn it!"

"He's back in the temporary cells, in the hangar." Batton pointed to the monitor, where the escapee was creeping out of an access door.

Deckard patted Mr. Batton on the shoulder. "I want all available men to the hangar at once. Take the bastard before he sets his friends free."

"Yes, sir," Mr. Batton said.

Deckard overlooked the *sir*, leaning in to study the monitor. The screen was only black and white, but he could see the prisoner clear as day. It was Bill Thompson.

Deckard's eyes flickered with the light of the screen. "Soon, you bastard, soon."

CHAPTER 27

Bill opened the service door a fraction of an inch and surveyed the hangar. Though he had been hesitant to use the service tunnels after his fight with the Customs dogs, he'd found he had little choice.

Soldiers were swarming through the terminal, leaving no hiding place untouched.

So he went back into the tunnels, praying he had seen the last of any stray animals. He had been fine, and he felt foolish for straying back into the terminal.

He watched two soldiers moving about the hangar, evidently guarding Marie and the others. One of them answered his radio, and waving to the other guard, he ran out of the hangar to the terminal. To help with the manhunt, Bill assumed.

Now the odds were better, one against one. Bill waited for the remaining guard to stroll to the far end of the hangar, and then he slipped through the door and duck-walked across the wide area toward the cells. A large pile of shipping crates sat near the cages, and Bill reached them without being spotted. In the rafters overhead, he spotted a camera moving back and forth on its mount, watching and sending everything it saw to the security base, to Deckard.

Bill ignored the camera and ran up to the end of the first cell as the guard returned, speaking into the two-way radio pinned to his shoulder.

Bill didn't like what had to happen next, but he had no choice. If the guard sounded an alarm, all his efforts would be for naught. He needed to take the man down ... and fast, before others arrived.

He stepped out of hiding and plunged the combat knife into the man's chest just below his ribcage, slicing upward.

The two men stood face to face, and Bill slowly laid the soldier on the ground. The man's lower body was covered in blood, and his eyes had glazed, looking but seeing nothing.

Bill held the man's hand as he tried to take another haggard breath. He couldn't be a day over twenty, and Bill's heart broke. Deckard was making him kill innocent soldiers, innocent kids who were only following orders.

"I'm dying, aren't I?" The soldier asked, as though he didn't quite believe what had happened to him.

"I'm afraid you are, son," Bill said softly. "Hopefully you shouldn't be feeling any pain now."

The soldier's eyes focused, and he saw Bill for the first time. "Pain? No, not really. Kind of numb, though. And it feels like I wet myself. Did I?"

Bill looked down and saw the wet spot, but he shook his head. "No, son, you're fine. You're going to die with dignity."

"That's good then. That's what my dad would have wanted." His eyes blurred again and he looked over Bill's shoulder. "I hear music. Do you hear music?" Then his head slumped to the side and his chest stopped moving.

Bill reached out and closed the man's eyes, realizing something had died inside himself as well.

He wiped his knife on the soldier's shirt and took the man's rifle. There would be time for reflection later if he and his friends made it out alive.

Bill stepped to the first cell and opened the door. It appeared to be empty, and he was about to go to the next one when Marie jumped out from beside the door, desperately scratching for his eyes.

"Whoa, wait, Marie! It's me—stop, damn it!"

She swatted him a few more times before she recognized him. "Bill? Oh my God, it's you!" She jumped into his arms. "The uniform—I thought you were one of them!"

He embraced her for a moment and then pulled away. "Look, let's save the hellos for later. Right now they know I'm here, and we need to go before there's a dozen soldiers in here."

She nodded. "Okay. The others, we have to free the others." Her eyes went wide when she saw Bill's bandaged wrist. "Your arm, Bill. Are you okay? It looks painful."

He chuckled. "Painful? Yeah, a little, but I'll live. Now let's open these cells; we don't have much time."

Marie went to Melissa's cell, and Bill released Tessa and the kids. Ten seconds later, everyone stood in front of the cells, preparing to leave.

"Where's Janice?" Melissa asked. "We have to find her."

"Janice is dead," Bill said briskly. "There's nothing we can do for her. Look, I'll explain later, but right now we need to move. Come on." He gave Melissa a quick push to get her going and then led everyone to the service door.

Bill stopped at the tunnel entrance and poked his head inside. No more feral dogs lying in wait. He pushed his friends into the corridor one after another.

When they were all in the tunnel, Bill picked up a piece of pipe lying on the ground, and after closing the door he jammed it through the handle.

"There was a camera on us the whole time, so they know where we are; we need to get as far away from here as fast as we can." He handed the dead soldier's rifle to Melissa. "Here, take this and keep it ready. There are stray dogs running around the tunnels, and God only knows what else, so shoot first and let God sort it out later. You know how to use this?"

She nodded, popped out the clip to make sure it was full, slapped it back in and charged the chamber. Then she ran to the front of the group, and Bill watched her go, impressed by her knowledge of firearms.

"So where do we go from here?" Marie asked as they started down the tunnel with Bill taking the rear.

He shrugged. "Marie, I have absolutely no goddamn idea. If you have any suggestions, now would be the time to share them. Actually, if anybody has an idea, sound off because I've got nothing. We're trapped in an airport with a bunch of heartless soldiers, and outside there are bloodthirsty killers who want nothing more than to tear us apart for the hell of it." He shook his head. "By the way, it looks like we are so screwed it's ridiculous."

"Shhh, the children, we need to stay positive for the children," Marie scolded him.

"Don't worry about me," Kenny said, his face set with grim determination. "I know what's going on and I'm ready to fight."

Bill patted the boy's shoulder. The kid had grown up a lot quicker than he might have in a normal world.

He looked down at Phillip and tried to smile. "Still, don't worry, guys. We'll get through this. After all, we've gotten this far," he half-joked.

"You mean like my brother Roger got this far, Mr. Thompson?" Phillip asked softly.

Bill rubbed the boy's shoulder. "Son, we wouldn't be here now if it wasn't for your brother, and don't you ever forget that."

Phillip smiled and nodded.

"Good. All right then, let's pick up the pace. And, Melissa, remember what I said."

She grunted, then turned back to watch their front. Bill let the rest go a few feet in front of him and glanced over his shoulder to make sure the tunnel was secure.

The soldiers were already banging on the service door behind him.

Setting his jaw in determination, he jogged to catch up to the others, praying a miracle would help them break free.

CHAPTER 28

The two-way radio crackled, and a man's voice floated from the small speaker. "There's no sign of the prisoners, Sergeant-Major, and we have another man down. Looks like he was stabbed."

"Dammit!" Deckard screamed into the radio. "Do you know where they went?"

"Ah, that's an affirmative. They ducked into the service tunnels that run parallel with the terminal. We should be able to pick up their trail just as soon as we get the door open. It seems blocked somehow."

"Enough! I don't want any more time wasted! Shoot the damn hinges off and find them—now!"

"Yes, Sergeant-Major." The radio went silent.

Deckard watched the monitors as two soldiers shot the hinges off the door. The security system had no sound, so he couldn't hear the shots or the clap of the heavy metal door hitting the ground, but he knew the prisoners must have heard. So much for the element of surprise.

While the service tunnels were internal, Deckard was fairly confident that the air integrity of the terminal would hold, but he wasn't about to take chances with the lives of his men. He had already lost far too many.

He set the two-way radio so that all channels would receive his signal. "Attention, this is Deckard. As of now we are in a Code Red lockdown. All available personnel should don gas masks before risk of contamination, over and out."

"Does that include us?" Mr. Batton asked.

"No, we're fine in here. This room has its own ventilation filters and seals around the doors. As long as that door stays closed, we're safe from the virus."

Batton and his partner Smith looked over to the metal security door that led into the terminal; the two-inch metal of the door suddenly seemed much too thin.

Deckard wandered away and started a discussion with a female soldier and an older man who was closer in rank to him than most of the men in the terminal, but Mr. Batton called him back almost immediately.

"What is it now, Batton? I'm trying to work out a strategy to find the prisoners."

"Um, sir, you should have a look at monitor four. You're not going to like it."

Deckard was about to scold Batton for calling him *sir*, but then his eyes lit up and his cigar fell from his mouth. "Oh my God, it can't be."

"I'm afraid it is, Sergeant-Major. There's an army out there and they're coming straight for us. Monitor four is about two miles out and was used for traffic control when the airport became congested. At the rate they're moving, they should be here in about a half hour." The man's voice was trembling by the time he finished.

Deckard stared at the flickering black-and-white screen. There were two men walking down the highway. One was young, with blond hair and a handsome physique. The other was an average-looking man with brown hair and a skinny frame. In itself, not so imposing. But behind the two men flowed a sea of people. Mr. Batton zoomed in on a few marchers in the crowd, and it was apparent they were infected. Their eyes were wide with rage and their mouths snapped at the empty air. With no sound coming from the screens, the procession of people possessed an almost ethereal quality.

Deckard fell back into his oversized chair. He dry-washed his face with his hands and let them fall to his lap. "After all we've fought through, to be taken down by a crowd of psychos."

"Seems like a lot more than a crowd out there, sir," Batton replied.

Deckard shot him a look that could have struck him dead.

Batton swallowed hard, deciding to change the subject quickly. "What are your orders, sir?" he asked, looking to Smith for moral support.

Smith was a quiet man who preferred to let Batton do the talking. Nobody usually shot the quiet guy when things fell apart.

Deckard snapped out of it and sat up in his chair. Standing, he walked back to the monitors and studied them again.

"I want all available men to the entrance of the airport. Use the Hummers and transport trucks to shore up the gate. As soon as the attackers are in sight, tell the men to fire. Aim for the head. Headshots will be better. Bring all heavy armaments, every damn grenade in the armory. If our perimeter is broken, we're all dead." He spoke the last five words slowly, with emphasis on each one.

"But what about the prisoners?" Mr. Batton asked.

"Fuck the prisoners. Besides, if those infected animals manage to get in here, the damn prisoners will be just as dead as the rest of us."

Deckard leaned forward and his eyes went wide when the man still didn't move. "Don't just sit there, son, get started!"

Batton jumped in his seat and grabbed the two-way radio sitting next to him. He ordered all personnel to the main gate.

Midway Airport was surrounded by water on two sides. High fences ran around the perimeter from the water to the highway and then continued around the airport to be lost from sight. Only from the main highway could you gain entrance.

The soldiers had made a temporary gate out of old fencing to block the highway, but it was nowhere up to the challenge of stopping the thousands of infected approaching the airport.

Their only hope was to block the entrance with the large trucks and use the M-60s to mow down any attacker stupid enough to attempt entry.

While soldiers ran about the terminal, now in gas masks, and trucks rolled across the tarmac to reach the gate, Deckard watched from the safety of his security base. He felt like Patton on the brink of a great battle.

He put another cigar in his mouth and glanced at the desk to the far right of Mr. Batton, focusing on the small red button under the glass cover. The demolitionist had jury-rigged the button soon after they arrived. It was a failsafe, connected to dozens of packages of C-4, all scattered across the terminal in key locations. If the airport was overrun and all hope was lost, Deckard would make sure that with his last breath he took all the infected to Hell with him.

He returned to his chair, making sure his gas mask still hung from its armrest. His hand went down to the Desert Eagle strapped snuggly to his hip.

All he could do was wait and let fate take its course.

CHAPTER 27

Bill called a halt when he saw a four-way junction at the far end of the tunnel. New corridors curved off to the left and right, so they had no way of knowing what lay around each bend.

"Shit, I have no idea where we should go," he said. "Any suggestions?"

"Maybe we should go back into the terminal and talk to someone," Melissa said. "Surely they'll listen to reason."

Bill snorted. "Oh yeah? And what should we say? Please, Mr. Sergeant Deckard, don't cut me up and dissect me. I don't think I'd like it."

Melissa crossed her arms and frowned. "Well, if you're going to say it like that, I agree it probably wouldn't work."

"No, it wouldn't, and I'll tell you why. I was the one who saw Janice spread out on a metal table with her chest peeled open like a chicken. These people are desperate, and they think we're the Holy Grail. We need to escape, and we need to do it as soon as possible." He looked over at Marie for her support, but she hadn't heard a word of it. She was hugging herself and staring at the wall across from her.

Bill laid a hand on her shoulder. "Hey, you all right? You look like you've just seen a ghost."

"Maybe I have. All our ghosts, in fact. Look, I don't expect you to believe me, but I get feelings sometimes. And I'll tell you what, I've got a feeling like some serious shit is coming down. Bill, we need to leave this place—fast."

"What the hell do you think we're doing? These damn tunnels are like a maze and we're the mice."

"What about that ladder?" Kenny asked from behind Melissa and Tessa. "Could we go up there?"

"What ladder?" Bill asked.

"There." Kenny pointed to a metal ladder set into the wall, almost hidden from Bill's angle. On closer inspection, he noticed a blue circle painted on the floor and ceiling. If he was right, the circles were for spotting the ladders before you came upon them.

"Where does it go?" Tessa asked, looking up into the alcove where the ladder disappeared into the ceiling.

"Well, boys and girls, there's only one way to find out." Bill started climbing. After the first ten rungs he was lost in darkness. He closed his eyes and waited a moment, and when he opened them again he could just make out the silhouette of the ladder. Climbing was difficult with his bad wrist, but he gritted his teeth and kept going.

Finally Bill reached a hatch. He tried to unlock it, wincing from the pain. He stopped and rested a moment.

"How's it coming?" Marie's voice echoed from below him. "Can we get out that way?"

"I don't know yet. It's either locked or stuck—it's hard to tell in the dark. Just give me another minute and I'll know for sure!"

Bill pulled out the combat knife. He wedged it into the latch and pried, wondering if the blade would give first and perhaps blind him with its shrapnel. He pushed the macabre thought away and focused on the lock. He shifted the blade a little to the right, and something snapped.

Involuntarily, he flinched, as if that would stop the exploding blade from piercing his eyelid. But the knife was fine; the latch had popped open.

Bill pushed up on the hatch with his head and shoulder and was surprised to be blinded by the afternoon sun.

Blinking away the spots of light, he stepped onto the large roof of the terminal, so large the edge wasn't easily discernable. He called to the others, and one at a time they made their way up the ladder, each one wincing from the bright sun. Bill shut the hatch behind them.

Marie took a deep breath and smiled. "Lord, that feels good. After being in that cell, I honestly wondered if I'd ever be outside again."

"Aww, it wasn't that bad," Phillip said with a grin.

Marie ruffled his hair and laughed. "Ah, youth, nothing bothers them."

"You know," Bill said, "when I cracked the hatch I destroyed whatever containment they had inside the terminal. The virus is probably already spreading in there right now."

"Who gives a shit?" Melissa asked. "Those bastards killed Janice and would have killed us too if you hadn't saved us!"

"Yes, Bill, you saved us," Marie said, kissing him on the cheek. "Again!"

He blushed for a second, unable to stop himself from smiling. But then he cleared his throat and tried his best to remain serious. "Let's see if there's a way off this roof. Maybe we can hijack a truck and run the gate."

"You mean just like in the movies when the good guys have to escape from the bad guy's headquarters?" Kenny asked excitedly.

Bill patted the boy's shoulder. "Exactly like that. And I'll need all hands to help me. Are you up for it? And you, too, Phillip?"

Both boys pumped their arms in the air and ran off to see if they could find a way down from the roof.

Bill glanced at Marie and saw the disapproval on her face. "What?" he asked innocently.

"You know what. Those boys are five and thirteen, and you want them running around the roof like commandos. What if Phillip falls off?"

Bill shrugged. "He'd die?"

Marie's frown grew deeper, and Bill waved his hand to calm her down. "I'm only joking. Look, Marie, for the moment it's a new world. Even the young ones have to learn to fight. Phillip will be fine. He's a tough one. You know that."

She sighed. "I know. It's just that I want to protect them. They've already been through so much."

"Maybe so, but I bet before we get away from here they'll have been through a lot more."

"I sure as hell hope not."

Across the roof, his body a small shape in the sunlight, Kenny began to jump up and down and wave his arms for attention. Phillip sprinted back from the other end to join him.

"See?" Bill said, starting off toward the boys. "I told you they could help."

Reluctantly, Marie followed him, and Tessa and Melissa, who had been talking softly together, moved across the roof with them as Kenny continued to jump up and down, waving for them to hurry.

CHAPTER 30

Dean slowed when the airport gate came into view at the end of the highway. Trucks and armed men lined the fence, using old shipping crates for support.

He chuckled, and Mike turned to see what was so funny. Dean pointed to the fence and sighed. "Look there, Mikey. Look what your pitiful friends are trying to do. They somehow think they have the power to stop me because they have weapons." Dean turned to the thousands behind him and raised his hands to the sky. "There aren't enough bullets in the entire state to stop us all! Am I right?"

The Infected shrieked and yelled and punched at the air.

Less than half a mile away, the soldiers on guard heard the chanting and screaming, and each one shuddered. Most of the men had been pulled from bureaucratic posts to fill the personnel roster when the outbreak started. None had been trained in battle.

"So you're just going to charge in there like cattle?" Mike asked. "You'll be mowed down. It'll be a slaughter."

"Oh no, on the contrary. True, the first wave will go down, but the others behind them will use their corpses for stairs and tear down the fence and kill all of those foolish soldiers. Then we'll find every normal and wipe them from existence." Dean turned to him. "What's wrong, Mikey? You don't look like you agree with my plan."

"No, it's fine. I can't say that I care either way. It's just ..."

"Yes, go on, spit it out."

"Well, it's just that if you're going to kill all the uninfected, where does that leave me?"

Dean nodded and placed a finger under his chin, as if thinking deeply. "Well, I wasn't rushing it, but you're right. If I want to kill all the normals, then I can't exactly let you live, now can I? I was going to wait until later, but I suppose now is as good a time as any."

Mike's eyes went wide. "What's a good time?"

Dean's mouth creased into a thin smile, his eyes gleaming maliciously. "Why, to say goodbye to you, Mike. I'm afraid you're no longer of use to me. Thanks for all the information. I really do appreciate it."

Dean directed three men and a woman to take Mike by the arms, and before Mike could protest, he was pulled into the crowd. He managed a few shocked screams before the infected ripped him apart, his arms going one way, his legs another. When there was nothing left but a bloody torso, some of the infected moved off to enjoy their prizes.

Dean watched with a solemn face. He saw a few of the Changed eating Mike's body parts, and he grimaced. "Disgusting. Killing him is one thing, but eating him? That's kind of ..." He mulled the next word over for a few seconds, then finished the sentence with a smile. "That's kind of right. I like it. What better way to destroy your enemy than to eat him?"

One of the Changed heard him and brought over what was left of Mike's left arm. Dean waved her away. "No thank you, dear, I had a big lunch. Maybe later."

The woman grunted and jumped around, waving the arm over her head and shaking blood all over the people around her before returning to her feast.

Dean turned back to the large gate blocking the highway. It was time.

He held out both arms to his sides and screamed at the top of his lungs, silencing his people. Then with an almost preternatural silence surrounding them, thousands of infected moved toward the airport in complete silence. Only their feet marching across the warm concrete could be heard.

CHAPTER 31

"Fantastic, Kenny," Bill said, slapping the boy on the back. "You found our way off the roof."

Below their feet, set into the wall, an emergency access ladder ran down the building to the tarmac below.

Kenny beamed with pride and Tessa nudged him. "Don't go getting all full of yourself," she joked. "Any idiot could have found it."

"Nonsense," Bill said, "he did great. Now let's get down from here and see about finding a truck or something and leaving this place behind."

Before the first person could start down the ladder, shots rang out from the far corner of the building, echoing from far away.

Bill and the others ran across the gravel roof to see what was happening. He felt a strange sense of déjà vu, thinking back to the school they had left behind, remembering the people they had lost since then, good men and women who had only wanted to survive, all gone.

"Oh my God!" Marie shouted as they reached the edge of the roof. "It can't be!" Bill could only watch, too awestruck to say anything.

Less than half a mile across the runway, a mass of people was attacking the gate. Already the perimeter fence was wobbling under their weight.

Soldiers fired into the mob, their machine guns popping like popcorn, their hand grenades detonating in bursts of light.

"What do we do now?" Melissa asked.

"There's so many of them," Tessa said softly. "There's no way those soldiers can stop them all."

Bill stepped in front of them, trying to block their view of the battle. "No, we didn't come this far to give up now. Listen, we can use this as a distraction to escape. The soldiers will be too busy dealing with this new threat to worry about us. So now is the time to get off this roof and find some way out of here. Are you guys with me?"

Marie placed her hand on his shoulder and smiled. "Of course we're with you, Bill. You've managed to get us this far, haven't you?"

He frowned. "I've lost a few on the way."

"That's not your fault, Bill," Melissa added. "Roger, Janice, Bruce—there was nothing you could do for them."

Marie nodded and smiled. "It's true, Bill. Don't beat yourself up. Frankly, I think it's a miracle any of us are still alive at all."

"And we're gonna stay that way," Bill said. "Come on, let's move out. Melissa, can I have that rifle?"

She shrugged. "Sure, I'm not that great a shot anyway."

Bill placed the rifle over his shoulder and cinched the strap tighter. "All right, I'll go down first and give you guys cover. Just give me a minute or two."

He started down the ladder. It wasn't a permanent fixture, just used for maintenance. The thin metal bent beneath Bill's weight. It was stronger than it looked, but he wasn't taking any chances. He went nice and slow. As the largest of their group, if he could make it down okay, the others would be fine. The screams and gunshots in the distance reminded him he needed to keep moving.

On the ground, he waved to the others. "Come on, it's a piece of cake!" Then he brought the rifle around to keep watch.

He was in the rear of the terminal. Luggage carts were spread about, and a few stair cars were parked in the corner. He could just see the wing of a large passenger plane. So far there was nothing that could be used as an escape vehicle.

Five minutes later, everyone was down. Marie took the longest. She looked to Bill bashfully. "Sorry I took so long. I'm a little afraid of heights."

He nodded. "You did great." Looking to his fellow survivors, he grinned. "Now let's get the hell out of here."

A smile lit up everyone's face, and with Bill in the lead, they started out onto the runway.

"Freeze!" someone shouted. "Or die where you stand!"

The survivors did as they were told, and Bill turned slightly to peek over his shoulder.

Three soldiers rushed toward them, hard grimaces of hate behind their gas masks.

"Drop your weapon—now!" the first soldier in line barked.

Bill did as he was ordered, the others standing still with their hands out to their sides.

"Now kick it over here," the soldier ordered.

With the tip of his foot, Bill gave the rifle a shove; it slid a few feet before the drag of the cloth strap slowed it.

The soldiers stopped at ten paces, holding their rifles at waist level. Bill could only pray none of them had itchy trigger fingers.

"You people are the prisoners everyone's been looking for." The soldier turned to Bill. "You killed a friend of mine at the lab, you bastard. I was hoping I'd get to pay you back for it." He gestured for Bill to step away from the others. "Over there. Move, or so help me I'll cut you and the others down together."

Marie held an arm out to Bill, but he pushed her away. "No, it's all right, he's right. I took lives I had no right taking."

"That's bullshit and you know it!" Melissa screamed. "Those pricks were trying to kill you and probably us, too. Look at what they did to Janice! They should all burn in Hell!"

"Shut the fuck up, lady, or you can join him," the soldier snapped through his gas mask.

Melissa quieted down, though her face still showed defiance. Phillip hugged Marie's legs. She patted his head and told him it would be all right.

Bill gestured with his chin toward the staccato of gunshots and shrieks coming from over the main terminal. "You hear that? There's a giant crowd of raving, murderous people coming through your little barricade, and once they get through, this place is going to be overrun."

"I don't give a flying fuck what happens to this place. There's nowhere to go anyway. And we can't wear these masks forever. We need to eat and drink. Once we take these off we'll become infected anyway."

"Then what's the point?" Marie asked.

"The point is that I can take you bastards with me; that's the fucking point!"

Bill said, "That's ridiculous. We're not infected. We can live through this!"

"And that sucks! Why do you get to live while so many of us die? Screw you! If I'm gonna die, then I'm taking you with me!"

Bill imagined a smile forming across the man's face, though with the mask on there was no way to tell.

"Don't worry, buddy, you won't be alone in Hell for long. Your friends will be joining you real soon. Well, maybe not the women," the soldier said heavily.

The other two soldiers laughed, and one of them rubbed his crotch.

"But you can't do that! If you do, you'll have to take off your masks," Melissa said.

The lead soldier stepped forward two steps. "I can do you just fine with the mask on. Sorry if you wanted me to kiss you."

The other soldiers laughed, and Melissa hugged herself as she thought of what was to come.

"Enough of this shit!" the second soldier yelled, his voice muffled under the mask. "Let's kill the bastard and have some fun."

"That's a damn good idea, Jake, a damn good idea." As one unit, the soldiers cocked their rifles.

Bill closed his eyes and waited for the crack of the rifles, the sharp pain of bullets ripping through him. Waiting for oblivion.

CHAPTER 32

Bill heard the rifles fire and braced himself. One bullet whizzed by his ear so close he felt it. A wide shot by a nervous soldier?

He'd always heard when you were about to die, your life flashed before your eyes, but all he could think of was the present, of how he wouldn't be around to see Phillip grow up or to help Marie lead the others. The face of his wife flickered briefly in his mind, and at least if he died, he would be with her again.

After taking three quick, panicked breaths, he cracked open his eyes. He should have been dead by now.

The three soldiers lay facedown on the tarmac, leaking blood from small wounds in their backs and from larger ones in their chests.

"What the hell?" Bill whispered.

From behind a stack of crates strode another soldier, the muzzle of his rifle still smoking. This man wasn't wearing a mask, but he was acting normal. His stride was purposeful and he held the rifle in his hand casually.

"Private Robinson?" Bill asked, surprised.

"Chris is better, but yeah, in the flesh. Hope you don't mind me helping out. It seemed you were in a little bit of a pickle."

Bill shook his head. "Um, no, of course not. Thank you. But why?"

"Well, what you said kept gnawing at me, and when I saw these three ready to gun you down it really hit home. If this is how we're supposed to save the world, by killing and torturing innocent people, well then maybe the world isn't worth saving."

"Amen to that, son," Marie said. She walked over and kissed him on the cheek. "Thank you for helping us. You're a life saver."

"Yeah, literally," Melissa added. "So has everybody forgotten, or are we going to wait for the party crashers to arrive?" She waved animatedly while she talked.

"Shit, she's right. Look, Chris, we're getting out of here, will you join us?" Bill asked.

"Sure, I'd be honored. Not like there's much of a future in the Army right now." He glanced down at the three dead soldiers. "I guess when I killed these guys I pretty much submitted my resignation."

"They're coming!" Kenny screamed, pointing to the far corner of the terminal.

"Shit, we need to go now or we're all dead!" Bill gathered the others into a group and started across the runway. Marie, Melissa and Tessa picked up the rifles of the dead soldiers, and Chris grabbed the spare clips.

Behind them, the first wave of infected rounded the corner of the main terminal and slowly spread out like African army ants. They ran around mindlessly, but it would only be a matter of seconds before they saw Bill and the others.

"What's the plan?" Chris asked, jogging next to Bill.

"No goddamn idea. I was hoping we could find a truck or van and use it to get out of here, but so far there's been nothing."

"And you won't find anything. All the transports were brought to the gate to reinforce it when we first spotted the army of infected. The sergeant-major sent all available personnel to fortify it. There's nothing left."

"What about hot-wiring something like they do in the movies?" Kenny asked.

"It's not that easy, kid," Chris replied. "In the movies, they pull a few wires and the engine starts, but in real life it's a little more complicated. Besides, I have no clue how to do it. Does anyone else?"

Bill and the others all shook their heads. They were all everyday people with normal jobs and families. There hadn't been many opportunities to learn how to hot-wire cars.

"Then we're screwed." Bill sighed long and loud. "Even if we run, they'll catch us eventually." He slowed down and the others followed suit. "What's the point? We have no transportation, and even if we did, the roads are jammed with wreckage and crazy people. It's hopeless."

"Wait," Chris said, "I've got an idea. Instead of driving out, why don't we fly out?"

"Fly? Sorry, Chris, but I left my pilot's license in my other jacket," Bill quipped.

Chris shook his head. "No, you don't understand. I can fly. Or I used to."

"Really? That's wonderful!" Marie exclaimed.

Chris held up his hands. "Now slow down; it was a few years ago. I took a few lessons in high school. They had a program when I was in Aviation Science." He pointed across the tarmac to a small Cessna hiding between two larger passenger planes. "I didn't know that was there, but if we can get it started, I should be able to fly it."

"Great," Tessa said, throwing her hands in the air. "Back to hot-wiring something. But now it's an airplane. And I'm sure that's much easier to hot-wire than a car."

"No time to discuss it now," Bill said; the first of the infected had spotted them and were sprinting toward them. "It's our best chance."

Chris nodded and the group started toward the Cessna. Bill sent a volley of bullets at the closest runners. One woman fell straight to the ground, her hands at her sides. Her face hit the tarmac, shattering her nose and breaking her teeth. She tried to stand again, her face a bloody mess, but the others trampled her, crushing her to a crimson pulp.

Bill nodded to himself, satisfied. The rest were still a little ways off, and he could only hope to give Chris the time he needed.

It was a double-wide twin-engine plane, and Chris clapped his hands. "Hot damn, this is a lot like what I used to fly, though a little bigger."

"That's good, right? It means we can all fit," Melissa said from his side.

Chris nodded. "Hope so. But it'll be tight. We'll have to wait and see." He opened the door to the cockpit and motioned for Tessa to open the rear side door. The others climbed inside one at a time.

Marie took the co-pilot's seat, her mouth hanging open as she stared at all the knobs and controls.

In the pilot's seat, Chris quickly felt all over the cockpit.

"What are you doing?" Marie asked.

"Looking for the keys. Most pilots leave the keys in the planes somewhere. That way if the plane needs to be moved, the keys are in it. Some pilots leave them just so they won't lose them." His eyes lit up as he pulled down the small visor and a set of keys fell into his lap. "Huh, guess I should have looked there first. I didn't think it would be that easy."

Outside, Bill fired round after round into the growing mob. More than thirty were running toward the plane, with hundreds just rounding the corner of the farthest building.

The rifle clicked empty. "I'm out!" Bill cried.

Chris slid open his side window and tossed out a fresh magazine. "A few more seconds and I should have us out of here."

Bill shook his head as he inserted the magazine. "I don't think we have a few seconds, but I'll do my best." Then he couldn't talk as he sent a hailstorm of bullets into the charging bodies.

Chris slid the key into the ignition and started flicking knobs and controls. He turned to Marie and grinned. "I guess we'll waive the preflight inspection."

She only stared at him, not quite getting the joke.

Melissa had jumped down from the back of the plane and was helping Bill keep the attackers at bay, firing her rifle continually.

Bill sent the last of his magazine into the screaming mob and then pushed Melissa toward the plane. "That's it, I'm out!"

She nodded and climbed into the plane as the twin motors surged to life. Just before Bill entered behind her, he caught sight of the wooden blocks behind the front wheels. He handed his rifle to Melissa and then dove under the plane.

He managed to throw the wooden blocks aside without any trouble, but as he backed out from under the plane, the first of the infected wrapped an arm around his throat. The man hadn't bathed in more than a week, and with the mixture of blood and feces on his pants, he was ripe.

Breathing through his mouth to keep from gagging on the smell, Bill bent at the waist and threw the man over his head. The attacker got back on his feet quickly, but this time Bill was prepared. He lunged forward and swiped with his combat knife. The man never slowed, either too stupid to fear the blade, or just indifferent to the danger thanks to the virus eating his brain.

Biting empty air and groping for Bill, the attacker ran directly into the knife. Bill pushed the blade in deeper and twisted it as he pulled it out.

The man stopped for a moment, looking down at the entrails spilling out of his body. Then he went after Bill again, unfazed.

A rifle cracked, muffled by the engines of the plane; the man's head snapped back as he crumpled to the tarmac. Two other infected came at Bill, and one at a time they fell to the tarmac, writhing from bullet wounds. Bill turned to see Melissa lowering the rifle.

He waved and ran up to the rear door of the Cessna. Melissa helped him inside, then slammed the door and secured the latch.

Out of breath, Bill leaned forward and whispered into Chris' ear. "Can we go now, please?"

Chris nodded and pushed the yoke forward, working the pedals with his feet. The engine revved louder, and the plane started moving, spraying blood and flesh across the tarmac as an attacker was caught in the whirling blades of the left engine.

Bill and the others cheered at the sight, but Chris frowned.

"What's wrong?" Marie asked from the passenger seat.

"The blades. It's not like in the movies. When a body gets caught up in the propellers, it could warp them or make them off balance. Shit, they can even snap off."

"But are we okay?" Marie asked, looking out the front window at the massive amount of people charging toward them.

"Think so. The blade only grazed that guy—we should be okay. If anything, I can fly on one engine."

Everyone remained silent as Chris started down the runway at about thirty miles per hour, maneuvering around crowds of screaming people, most covered in blood as if someone had dumped can after can of red paint on them.

Bill reloaded his rifle and opened the rear door to take potshots at the closest attackers. The cool breeze dried the sheen of sweat on his brow.

Dropping one hostile after another, he quickly realized it was futile—he could never kill them all—but every attacker he took down was one less to block the plane. So he kept firing as

Chris zigzagged around the throngs, hoping it would be enough to get them to the runway, hoping it was enough to get them somewhere safe.

CHAPTER 33

"Report, goddammit!" Deckard screamed into the two-way radio. "What the hell is happening out there?"

More than five minutes had passed since the last check-in, and despite his demands, no one was answering.

Dropping the radio, he turned to look at the monitors. The small screens showed a massacre of unbelievable proportions. Bodies were piled dozens high in front of the gate, and many of the soldiers lay dead or dying under a swarm of men and women.

When one of the transport trucks blew up in a fireball of orange and reds, Deckard actually backed away from the screen, almost as if the image could burn. The flames turned into a ball of smoke, which the wind cut to ribbons. When enough cleared that he could see the gate again, he wasn't pleased.

The chain link fence, more than twenty feet high, plus barbed wire, was knocked over on both sides of the highway, trampled into the grass. Bodies were everywhere, some twitching or crawling, most immobile.

Deckard zoomed in on the gate to find every last one of his men dead. Weapons were scattered across the gravel and pavement; the infected had no need for them.

He watched as a man slowed down and looked directly into the camera. This man seemed different, almost normal. He wasn't running around like a raving lunatic, but was calmly surveying the carnage around him.

Deckard moved the camera to get a closer look. The man raised his right hand and flipped him off. Deckard's jaw dropped at the sight.

"What a cheeky bastard," Mr. Smith said as he watched the screen.

Deckard glared at him. "Shut up and do your job, dammit! What is the status of the infected mob? Do we still have containment?"

Mr. Smith sat up straighter and sort of nodded. "Um, well, we sort of do."

"What the hell does that mean? Do we or don't we have containment!"

"It'll be easier if I just show you, sir." Smith tapped his keyboard and changed some of the monitor screens, flicking to an outside view of the terminal. Crowds were banging on the doors, using steel pipes and rifles as clubs. The thick reinforced glass was holding up, but it wouldn't last.

"See? They're not in yet, but it's just a matter of time. We need to evacuate, sir. As soon as possible."

Mr. Batton nodded in agreement.

Deckard ignored him. "Evacuate? And just where the hell would we go? This is already our fallback camp. No one's answered us from Washington. The whole damn country is infected. No, we stay here and battle to the death. It's what any good soldier would do."

Mr. Batton looked up meekly from his chair. "But, sir, I'm a civilian. I'm only contracted to run the software. So is Smith."

Smith nodded, deciding if there was ever a time to speak up, this was it.

"I don't give a goddamn whether you're Army or not. As of now, you're all enlisted, and if you don't like it, tough shit. Besides, I don't think those people out there really care whether you're enlisted or not, do you?"

Both men looked at the monitors, at all the crazy, enraged faces, and then shook their heads. Those people out there didn't care about anything.

"All right then. We should be safe here for a while. Maybe we can hold out until help arrives ... if it ever comes. But we have no choice, gentlemen; we're in it for the long haul."

Deckard turned and waved to his aide and another soldier, a woman with short brown hair and glasses. Both came to him immediately, and he spoke in low whispers that neither Smith nor Batton could hear. When Deckard was done, the soldiers moved to their desk at the back of the room.

Looking back at the two security officers, Deckard smiled. "Don't worry, gentlemen, we're the United States Army, the most powerful military fighting machine on the planet. We'll prevail, we always prevail." Then he walked away to sit in his chair, relighting his cigar as he went.

Batton leaned close to Smith and whispered, "The mighty Army never fails, he said. Then what about Vietnam and Iraq, to name a few?"

"Shut up, man," Smith said quietly. "Don't let him hear you bad-mouthing the Army. The man's losing it. If I thought I could get out of here without him shooting me, I'd already be gone."

"You're not serious, are you?"

"Just look at his face and you tell me."

Batton turned in his chair slightly, trying not to attract Deckard's attention. He watched as the sergeant-major caressed his Desert Eagle, mumbling nonsense to himself. Smith was right. They were trapped between a madman and a pack of lunatics.

Altogether, he couldn't think of a worse day in his life, and he wished he could just go back to bed and start over.

Dean stopped at the entrance to the airport and surveyed the death and destruction. The smell of blood was in the air, urging him to run into the fray and rip and rend with his brethren. But he knew he was better than that. He looked up at a mounted camera as it moved back and forth. Someone was watching, someone who would be dead very soon.

Dean flipped off the camera, showing his best smile. Then he moved off, stepping over pieces of bodies. A man in an Army uniform groaned off to his right. Dean walked over to him, and the man reached out, his mouth opening and closing and drooling blood.

Dean squatted over the soldier's body, and with a hand on either side of his head, he twisted until he heard a snap. He wiped the bloody drool off his hand onto the man's uniform before wandering away.

His followers were well ahead of him, but Dean preferred to take his time and relish his victory. Once all the normals in the airport were slaughtered, he could move on to the next state. He had heard Indiana was nice this time of year.

Whistling, Dean strode down the highway into the airport, enjoying the day and the carnage to follow.

Off in the distance, the inferno that was once Chicago lit the broken horizon with orange and red, choking the sky with black smoke, snuffing out the sun like the hand of God.

CHAPTER 34

"Hold on!" Chris yelled, turning the yoke hard to avoid a large group of the infected. The plane leaned to the right, and the engines whined as Chris increased speed.

So far they had been unable to reach the runway. The tarmac was now almost completely full of mad, screaming people.

Bill emptied the rifle and closed the door. He had more ammo, but it was useless and dangerous. He ran the risk of being pulled from the plane.

The Cessna bounced and wobbled as Chris mowed down another person.

"This isn't working!" Bill yelled over the sound of the engines. "We need something to distract them long enough to make it to the runway!"

"What the hell do think I've been trying to do?" Chris asked. "They're everywhere. And if too many hit the propellers, they'll warp or break for sure!" He slammed the yoke to the left, avoiding a knot of people. A few had climbed onto the wings, and once the ride smoothed out, they began to crawl toward the cockpit.

Marie looked to the terminal. The doors were shattered and hundreds of people were flooding inside, the few remaining soldiers trying valiantly to hold them off.

"They're in the terminal," Marie said, barely loud enough to be heard over the engines.

Chris caught the end of her statement and glanced across the tarmac. "That's it then. There's no turning back. We either get this baby off the ground or we're dead."

Everyone looked up as footsteps pounded across the roof of the plane. Melissa yelled something and raised the rifle to shoot through the ceiling.

"No, you idiot!" Chris shouted. "This isn't a car! If you put holes in the plane it won't pressurize properly and it'll cause problems."

"Pressurize? It's a damn Cessna! Even I know we don't go that high!" she screamed back, her finger on the trigger.

"Yeah, but every hole will just add to the drag, and we could even rupture. So please don't shoot any holes in my plane!"

Chris pressed the breaks and the plane jolted to a stop for a fraction of a second. The man on the roof flew into the air as if he had been shot from a catapult, and he knocked over a large group of infected. Chris swerved to the right, avoiding the mass of arms and legs, winging one man with the left propeller.

"What's going to happen to all the soldiers inside the airport?" Tessa asked. Phillip had his head tucked into her chest, terrified by the noise and the screaming. On the seat next to them, Kenny was more controlled as he watched the tarmac through a small window, amazed at the ferocity of the people trying to get at them. Only thirteen, he felt immortal; he didn't fully comprehend that he could die.

Chris, still driving in circles, desperately trying to reach the runway, shrugged at Tessa's question. "Probably be killed or infected themselves. Once the containment seals were broken, anyone without a mask on was probably infected."

"You don't have a mask on," Kenny stated.

Everyone's face in the plane lit up, and Chris looked back at them. "Jesus, I hadn't given it much thought."

"You must be immune like us," Bill said. "Lucky Deckard didn't find out, or it might've been you on one of those surgical tables. By the way, I never thanked you for helping me escape. If you hadn't left one of my straps a little loose ..."

Chris nodded. "No problem. Glad it all worked out."

"You and me both," Bill said with a smile.

"It didn't work out for Janice," Melissa said.

"And I'm truly sorry for that, but I did what I could."

Bill stared at her. "Lay off him, Melissa. Let him concentrate on flying."

The plane slammed to the right and Chris put the terminal behind him again. The engines whined as he powered forward. "Hold on! I've got a small opening and I'm going for it!"

"Can we make it?" Marie asked from his side.

As if in answer, a clump of people closed the gap two hundred feet ahead.

CHAPTER 35

"They're here!" screamed Batton, turning his chair toward the security door that led into the terminal.

"No shit," Deckard said. Gripping his sidearm, comforted by the cool metal, the sergeant-major waited for the seals of the door to give out under all those bodies.

The far right monitor showed the security door from the outside, the mass of people banging on it, some crushed as their brethren pushed forward. The other monitors in the terminal showed the same thing. The infected were everywhere, overrunning his soldiers, trashing the research lab.

The door buckled inward, and Deckard donned his gas mask. He told the others to do the same. "And have your weapons ready. The second that door opens, start firing. Maybe we can hold them off."

"Not bloody likely," Smith said. He tried to count the number of lunatics outside the door and gave up after reaching a hundred. "We are so fucked."

Batton finished securing his mask and looked at Smith. "Come on, man, put your mask on. They'll be in here any second!"

"What's the point? Hell, maybe it won't be so bad to be one of them. They don't seem too unhappy."

Batton pulled out his gun. All personnel were armed, civilian or not. "Whatever, man, do what you want. Me, I'm gonna make it out of here in one piece."

Smith chuckled. "You just keep thinking that."

The door jumped in its frame, and Deckard noticed a ray of outside light seeping in.

"Shit, that's it, men. Containment breach. I want a firing line over here, now!"

All seven soldiers assumed their positions and aimed their weapons at the shaking door. Three were on their knees, and the others stood behind them, ready to fire over the heads of their comrades.

Smith just sat in his chair, smiling. The virus was already affecting him.

"Smith," Deckard said, "what the hell are you doing? Get into the firing line—they're almost in!"

"If it's all the same to you, sir, I think I'll sit this one out. I'd like to live my last few minutes free, not working for an asshole like you."

Deckard's eyes went wide behind his mask, but before he could reprimand the security guard, the door finally succumbed and fell in with a crash. Screaming men and women poured through the doorway like water through a broken dam.

"Fire at will!" Deckard screamed, and the room filled with the thunder of guns.

Faces exploded, arms were blown off and blood sprayed everywhere. Bodies piled up like cordwood.

Deckard reloaded. A crazed woman was only two feet away when he raised his weapon and blew off her head.

One after another, the infected poured into the control room. They could only attack in twos or threes, bottlenecked by the doorway, and Deckard used this to his advantage.

"I'm out, Sergeant-Major!" screamed one of the soldiers kneeling below him.

"Me too," one of his aides yelled over the deafening gunfire and the cries of the infected.

Smith sat quietly in his chair, as if watching an action movie. He only wished he had some popcorn.

Deckard fired his last round and reached in his belt for more ammo—but there was no more; he was empty.

Throwing the Desert Eagle at the closest attacker, he backed away from the firing line. One at a time, his men ran out of firepower, and the ones in front were overwhelmed by the intruders.

The crazies piled atop Batton, and his screams were muffled under his gas mask. So far they ignored Deckard, who had retreated to the security desk. Then he saw a blur to his right and a figure plowed into him. He looked down to see Smith, a feral grin on his face, trying to pull him to the floor.

"Smith, get a hold of yourself! What the hell are you doing?"

But Smith was oblivious, another killing machine. He sank his teeth into Deckard's arm and ripped the gas mask from his face. The sergeant-major screamed as he breathed in contaminated air. He pushed Smith away, losing a piece of his arm in the process.

He saw his soldiers were all dead or dying, one of them reaching out from the mass of bodies, groping for something, anything at all before his arm slackened and dropped away. Then Deckard was being pulled down too.

Hands ripped at his clothing as he pulled his combat knife from his belt and swiped blindly, slicing flesh. He had no way of knowing what damage he was inflicting, but he continued to slash until his knife stuck in bone and was pulled from his grip.

Someone yanked his arm out of the socket. Teeth found his leg, and his vision grew dim from the pain.

He was thrown across the security desk, and as he tumbled, he glimpsed the red button. He let out a bark of laughter that quickly turned to shrieks of pain.

He managed to free his left hand, and with one smooth motion he slammed his fist into the glass casing over the button. Glass shattered and lodged in his knuckles, but he didn't notice.

Below the button, a digital display flashed zero; two minutes appeared on the screen, and the red number started ticking down.

"Ha, you bastards, I win! Kill me if you want to, but I win!" Deckard's laughter mixed with his shrieks of agony.

An elderly woman darted in under his guard and bit his nose. He headbutted her, knocked her back. She took his nose with her. Blood poured into his nasal cavity and he began to choke, spitting blood at his attackers.

Five seconds remained on the counter.

"See you in Hell, you fuckers!" Deckard yelled at the top of his lungs. "I'll be waiting for you!"

A blinding flash filled the room and surrounding terminal. The entire Midway Airport had been wired with C-4, and one after another, the blasts ripped through the building, taking out support columns as they went. The inferno detonated two refueling trucks full of jet fuel and when the gas lines ruptured below the tarmac, the entire complex went up like a small sun.

Everything in a half-mile radius was incinerated immediately, and as the wave of living Hell rushed across the runway, a small Cessna valiantly tried to outrun it.

CHAPTER 36

"Oh my Lord!" Marie screamed. Behind them, the terminal had gone up in a fireball.

"Uh, Chris," Bill said, trying to keep the panic out of his voice, "I really think now would be a good time to go faster."

Chris took his eyes off the large group of infected blocking the runway; his jaw dropped when he noticed the explosion. "Oh shit, the crazy bastard did it!"

"Did what?" Bill cried.

"I heard rumors that Deckard rigged the entire airport with explosives, but I never actually believed he did it. You know, guys like to make shit up!"

"Well, he *did* do it—so for the love of God, hurry up!" Bill screamed.

The first tendrils of fire licked at the rudder of the Cessna. Chris tried to coax more power from the engines, but they were already at their maximum output. They wouldn't make escape velocity in time. Not with the human roadblock ahead. The plane, propellers first, would plow into the mass of bodies, spraying blood and bone before coming to a halt in the midst of the fireball. Bill and the others would be burned alive.

Then multiple things happened at once. The heat of the explosion burst past the aircraft and enveloped the mass of infected blocking the runway. The crazies ran, trying to escape the scorching air as their skin boiled and crisped. Even under the influence of the virus, it seemed they still possessed some sense of survival instinct.

But some ignored the heat, and with melting faces and burning hair, they charged the Cessna.

Protected from the heat, the plane rode the thermals of the blast, just staying out of reach of the fireball. Chris felt the wheels of the plane lift off the tarmac, and he pulled back on the yoke in an attempt to take flight. Tendrils of the massive explosion wrapped around the rudder, caressing the fiberglass, scorching the paint. Then the plane soared into the air and out of the inferno.

Chris banked the Cessna high, and when he reached a safe altitude, he turned to survey the airport. Secondary explosions rumbled through the complex, each terminal collapsing under the residual blasts from the gas mains. Only a few bodies were visible, all lying on the pavement. But soon those were lost in a giant smoke cloud so large it snuffed out even the sun. The plane cleared the perimeter and shot out into clear sky.

"Jesus, that was close," Bill muttered.

Chris nodded. "You know, if we hadn't gotten that extra boost from the explosion and the crowd hadn't opened up when it did, we never would have made it. Deckard saved our lives by setting off those explosives."

"No shit? Son of a bitch tries to kill me and ends up saving my ass." Bill saluted the flames below him. "To you, Sergeant-Major Deckard." He turned the salute into a middle finger. "Thanks for nothing, asshole."

"Bill, stop that," Marie said.

Bill looked ashamed. "Sorry, Marie, but the guy deserves it."

"Maybe, but he's dust now, so let it be, okay?"

"Sure, Marie, okay." He turned to Kenny and Phillip and tousled the smaller boy's hair. "Well, guys, what do you think?"

Kenny shrugged. "No biggy. I knew we were gonna make it all the time."

Bill chuckled, and soon the others laughed with him, just glad to be alive.

When the laughter died down, Bill turned back to Chris. "So what now? Any suggestions? After all, you're the pilot."

Chris furrowed his brow. "Well, we've almost got a full tank, so fuel is good. The rudder's a little sluggish, but still works. Probably damaged in the explosion. So I don't know. Where do you want to go?"

"How about Indiana?" Melissa suggested. "Maybe it's not so bad there. And if it is, we could just keep going."

No one objected.

"Indiana it is," Bill said.

Chris nodded and banked the plane west. They had maps, and once Chris was situated, he would have Marie calculate how far their fuel would get them.

The sun was just beginning to set, painting the sky a molten red, and soon the small aircraft was swallowed by the horizon, abandoning the charred remains of Chicago for a brighter future.

EPILOGUE

A few slabs of concrete had landed in such an angle that had protected Dean from being squashed. The raging fireball had washed over him, singing his flesh but not killing him.

With smoking clothes and a few minor burns, he pulled himself free of his rubble prison and looked out at the airport, now just a smoking crater. Most of the secondary explosions had stopped, but a steady fire still burned, fueled by the underground gas mains.

On wobbly legs, Dean stumbled around the blast site. He heard a low moan to his left and moved toward it. Five minutes later, after clearing away some rubble, he unearthed one of the Changed. The man had an ugly head wound, but was otherwise unhurt.

Dean helped him to his feet and brushed the ash from his clothes. "There you go, fella," he said, patting him on the back. "Let's see if we can find anyone else, hmm?"

Moving about the debris of shattered concrete and steel, Dean found four more of his people. One, a young woman in her late twenties, had lost all of her hair in the heat; even her eyebrows had been singed away. Her skin was a bright red, and Dean had the urge to slap her like you did when someone had a bad sunburn.

The other three people were just as badly injured. One had a dislocated shoulder, and Dean managed to pop it back into its socket.

No one else was alive, or if they were, they were in such bad shape they wouldn't be alive for long.

Dean looked up as a small airplane flew by overhead. He didn't know where the plane had come from and frankly didn't care.

"Well, folks," he said to his gathered followers, "it looks like you're it. Four. Just four people out of thousands, all gone in a flash." He sighed. "Oh well. Guess you have to start somewhere, right?"

In a single-file line, they followed him over the debris-strewn runway, shuffling along like drunks. They reached the highway, and a few hours later Dean spotted a green sign for Indiana. The exit was only half a mile away.

His plan was still the same. There would be more Changed in other cities, and he would recruit them, start over again. Indiana would be a great start.

Trying to whistle through sun-parched lips, Dean continued onward with a smile, his teeth flashing in the fading light. He wasn't finished with mankind. Not by a long shot.

AFTER TWILIGHT
WALKING WITH THE DEAD
by Travis Adkins

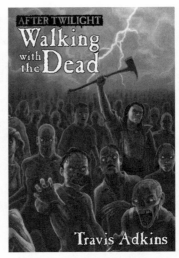

At the start of the apocalypse, a small resort town on the coast of Rhode Island fortified itself to withstand the millions of flesh-eating zombies conquering the world. With its high walls and self-contained power plant, Eastpointe was a safe haven for the lucky few who managed to arrive.

Trained specifically to outmaneuver the undead, Black Berets performed scavenging missions in outlying towns in order to stock Eastpointe with materials vital for long-term survival. But the town leaders took the Black Berets for granted, on a whim sending them out into the cannibalistic wilderness. Most did not survive.

Now the most cunning, most brutal, most efficient Black Beret will return to Eastpointe after narrowly surviving the doomed mission and unleash his anger upon the town in one bloody night of retribution.

After twilight,
> when the morning comes and the sun rises,
> will anyone be left alive?

ISBN: 978-1934861035

Drop Dead Gorgeous
by Wayne Simmons

As tattoo artist Star begins to ink her first client on a spring Sunday morning, something goes horribly wrong with the world... Belfast's hungover lapse into a deeper sleep than normal, their sudden deaths causing an unholy mess of crashing cars, smoldering televisions and falling aircraft.

In the chaotic aftermath a group of post-apocalyptic survivors search for purpose in a devastated city. Ageing DJ Sean Magee and shifty-eyed Barry Rogan find drunken solace in a hotel bar. Ex-IRA operative Mairead Burns and RIR soldier Roy Beggs form an uneasy alliance to rebuild community life. Elsewhere, a mysterious Preacher Man lures shivering survivors out of the shadows with a promise of redemption.

Choked by the smell of death, Ireland's remaining few begin the journey toward a new life, fear and desperation giving rise to new tensions and dark old habits. But a new threat--as gorgeous as it is deadly--creeps slowly out of life's wreckage. Fueled by feral hunger and a thirst for chaos, the corpses of the beautiful are rising...

ISBN: 978-1934861059

Permuted Press
The formula has been changed...
Shifted... Altered... *Twisted.*™
www.permutedpress.com

DYING TO LIVE
LIFE SENTENCE
by Kim Paffenroth

At the end of the world a handful of survivors banded together in a museum-turned-compound surrounded by the living dead. The community established rituals and rites of passage, customs to keep themselves sane, to help them integrate into their new existence. In a battle against a kingdom of savage prisoners, the survivors lost loved ones, they lost innocence, but still they coped and grew. They even found a strange peace with the undead.

Twelve years later the community has reclaimed more of the city and has settled into a fairly secure life in their compound. Zoey is a girl coming of age in this undead world, learning new roles—new sacrifices. But even bigger surprises lie in wait, for some of the walking dead are beginning to remember who they are, whom they've lost, and, even worse, what they've done.

As the dead struggle to reclaim their lives, as the survivors combat an intruding force, the two groups accelerate toward a collision that could drastically alter both of their worlds.

ISBN: 978-1934861110

EDEN
A ZOMBIE NOVEL BY TONY MONCHINSKI

Seemingly overnight the world transforms into a barren wasteland ravaged by plague and overrun by hordes of flesh-eating zombies. A small band of desperate men and women stand their ground in a fortified compound in what had been Queens, New York. They've named their sanctuary Eden.

Harris—the unusual honest man in this dead world—races against time to solve a murder while maintaining his own humanity. Because the danger posed by the dead and diseased mass clawing at Eden's walls pales in comparison to the deceit and treachery Harris faces within.

ISBN: 978-1934861172

Permuted Press
The formula has been changed...
Shifted... Altered... Twisted.™
www.permutedpress.com

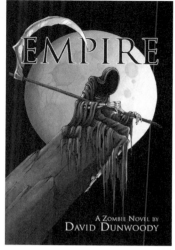

Day by Day Armageddon

by J. L. Bourne

An ongoing journal depicting one man's personal struggle for survival, dealing with the trials of an undead world unfolding around him. An unknown plague sweeps the planet. The dead rise to claim the Earth as the new dominant species. Trapped in the midst of a global tragedy, he must make decisions... choices that that ultimately mean life, or the eternal curse to walk as one of them.

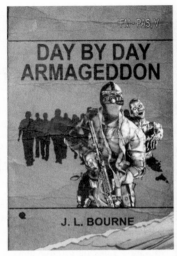

ISBN: 978-0-9789707-7-2

EVERY SIGH, THE END.
(A novel about zombies.)
by Jason S. Hornsby

It's the end of the world: 1999.

Professional nobody Ross Orringer sees flashes of cameras and glances from strangers lurking around every corner.

His paranoia mounts when his friends and family begin acting more and more suspiciously as the New Year approaches.

In the last minutes before the clock strikes midnight, Ross realizes that the end may be more ominous than anyone could have imagined: decisions have been made, the crews have set up their lights and equipment, and the gray makeup has been applied.

In the next millennium, time will lose all meaning, and the dead will walk the earth.

ISBN: 978-0-9789707-8-9

Permuted Press
The formula has been changed...
Shifted... Altered... Twisted.™
www.permutedpress.com

HISTORY IS DEAD

A ZOMBIE ANTHOLOGY EDITED BY
KIM PAFFENROTH

"History is Dead is a violent and bloody tour through the ages. Paffenroth has assembled a vicious timeline chronicling the rise of the undead that is simultaneously mind-numbingly savage and thought provoking."

—Michael McBride, author of the *God's End* trilogy and *The Infected*

ISBN: 978-0-9789707-9-6

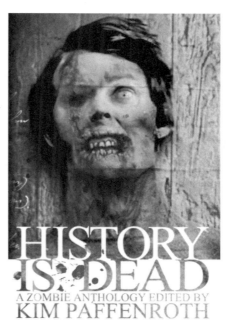

ROSES OF BLOOD ON BARBWIRE VINES

D.L. Snell

As the living dead invade a barricaded apartment building, the vampire inhabitants must protect their human livestock. Shade, the vampire monarch, defends her late father's kingdom, but Frost, Shade's general, convinces his brethren to migrate to an island where they can breed and hunt humans. In their path stands a legion of corpses, just now evolving into something far more lethal, something with tentacles —and that's just the beginning.

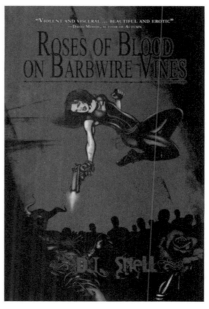

ISBN: 978-0-9789707-1-0

MORE DETAILS, EXCERPTS, AND PURCHASE INFORMATION AT
www.permutedpress.com

ISBN: 978-0-9765559-6-4

Twilight of the Dead
BY TRAVIS ADKINS

Five years after the dead first walked, a small pocket of humanity survives in the fortified town of Eastpointe.

When a stranger arrives claiming to know the location of a cure for the zombie plague, the town will risk everything to possess it.

But does the cure even exist?
And what price must be paid?

"If you love zombies, this is a must-read."
—Nickolas Cook, *Hellnotes*

THE OBLIVION SOCIETY
by Marcus Alexander Hart

Life sucks for Vivian Gray.
She hates her dead-end job.
She has no friends.

Oh, and a nuclear war has just reduced the world to a smoldering radioactive wasteland.

Armed with nothing but pop-culture memories and a lukewarm will to live, Vivian joins a group of rapidly mutating survivors and takes to the interstate for a madcap cross-country road trip toward a distant sanctuary that may not, in the strictest sense of the word, exist.

ISBN 978-0-9765559-5-7

THE
UNDEAD
ZOMBIE ANTHOLOGY
ISBN: 978-0-9765559-4-0

"Dark, disturbing and hilarious."
—Dave Dreher, *Creature-Corner.com*

THE
UNDEAD
VOLUME 2
SKIN AND BONES
ISBN: 978-0-9789707-4-1

"Permuted did us all a favor with the first volume of *The Undead*. Now they're back with *The Undead: Skin and Bones*, and gore hounds everywhere can belly up to the corpse canoe for a second helping. Great stories, great illustrations... *Skin and Bones* is fantastic!"
—Joe McKinney, author of *Dead City*

The Undead / volume three
FLESH FEAST
ISBN: 978-0-9789707-5-8

"Fantastic stories! The zombies are fresh... well, er, they're actually moldy, festering wrecks... but these stories are great takes on the zombie genre. You're gonna like *The Undead: Flesh Feast*... just make sure you have a toothpick handy."
—Joe McKinney, author of *Dead City*